INTRUDING THOUGHTS . . .

When I opened my office door, I could see my friend Franny wasn't in the waiting room, which nearly gave me both a migraine and a panic attack, till I saw the note taped to the back of one of the chairs.

Bored to death, it read. *Went to Meg's restaurant. I'll meet you there. Franny.*

By the time I double-locked the door to my office, I was looking forward to a nice relaxing lunch and an ice-cold glass of Chablis. I walked through the waiting room, snagging my coat off the coatrack as I passed.

I was halfway to the door and half into my coat before it registered. I stopped dead, heart pounding like a percussion band in my ears, and turned back. There on the upper protrusion of the coatrack pole, the part that flares out above the hooks, drawn in white chalk, was a four-pointed star. The crudely sketched monkey in the center had its paws over its ears.

The killer had been here, right here in my office!

Carrie Carlin mysteries by Nancy Tesler

PINK BALLOONS AND OTHER DEADLY THINGS

SHARKS, JELLYFISH AND OTHER DEADLY THINGS

SHOOTING STARS AND OTHER DEADLY THINGS

SHOOTING STARS

✴ AND ✴

OTHER DEADLY THINGS

A CARRIE CARLIN MYSTERY

NANCY TESLER

A Dell Book

Published by
Dell Publishing
a division of
Random House, Inc.
1540 Broadway
New York, New York 10036

ISBN: 0-440-22614-7

Printed in the United States of America

Published simultaneously in Canada

April 1999

10   9   8   7   6   5   4   3   2   1

WCD

This book is dedicated with love to my sons,
Ken, Bob, and Doug

Acknowledgments

The author wishes to thank the following people who, especially during those terrifying "blocked" times, offered encouragement, advice, information, and constructive criticism; the incomparable Ann Loring, the Roundtable Writers, Karen Sabine, Bob Tesler, Amy Miale, Sophida Thaitae and family, Joan and Bernie Sheffler, and Mike Friedman.

Special thanks to my friend and fellow writer, Tom Rooney, who surfed the Net for me in places I still dare not venture, to Sergeant Pete Mezey and Patrolman John Trainor of the Tenafly Police Department, and to my agent, Grace Morgan, for her continuing support and friendship.

At Dell, I'd like to express my gratitude and appreciation to my astute editor, Jackie Farber, to my ever-vigilant copyeditor, Kathy Lord, and to Mike Wepplo, who gets inside my head and keeps creating these imaginative eye-catching covers.

1

*

I AM ENCASED *in billowing clouds of tulle and lace. Cumbrous Scarlett O'Hara skirt anchors me, snug bodice crushes my ribs. A filmy veil obscures the pearl choker encircling my neck.*

"Exquisite," pronounces saleslady number one. "Like an angel."

"Five thousand," trumpets saleslady wo. "A bargain."

"No!" I cry, ripping off the veil and tearing at the necklace. "Choking me. Can't breathe. Take it off!"

"Take it, take it," chorus the salesladies, closing in. "Buy now, pay later. Marry now, pay later."

"Please. Suffocating. Can't breathe," I gasp as—

—the alarm's caterwaul blasted me awake. Wrenching the pillow off my face, my hand flailed around, snared the offender, and smothered it mute.

"Breathe," I commanded myself as I struggled to quiet

1

my thudding heart. "Breathe." Several deep diaphragmatic breaths later, I felt the oxygen rush as my muscles relaxed. A rough feline tongue began sandpapering the skin off my neck, while a hundred and five pounds of canine shifted position, nailing my feet to the bed. I groaned, pried my eyes open, and squinted at the daylight sifting through the blinds. No sun. It was one of those blustery fall days that strip the leaves from the trees, leaving them bare and exposed like undressed mannequins in a store window.

I am not a morning person. I rarely wake up overflowing with the milk of human kindness—especially after a night when I'd lain awake till two trying to balance income against outgo and coming up short. The rest of the night was a jumble of disconnected dreams, the kind, like the last, that filter in and out of your consciousness and leave you feeling trashed in the morning like a college freshman after a frat party.

I kicked off the covers. Horty whined in protest as he hit the floor. Patting his rump apologetically, I yelled to the kids to rise and shine. Well, at least rise and throw on some clothes, shining not being a requirement and certainly not on my agenda this dismal Thursday morning. Yawning, I made it to the bathroom, splashed my face with cold water, and did a half-baked job with the rest of my ablutions. Followed by the four members of our live-in menagerie, I trudged downstairs to get breakfast started. The phone rang just as the kettle whistled. I opened the back door to let Horty out, got blown back inside, and caught it on the fourth ring. "Hullo," I grunted.

"And aren't we in a happy mood this morning, my sweet."

"It's six-you-know-what-thirty in the morning, I had a horrible dream, and I haven't had my coffee yet."

"Uh-oh. Maybe I should call back. My news isn't going to improve things."

"Tell me now. Make my day." I poured boiling water into my instant coffee and took a life-affirming sip.

"Have to take a rain check for the weekend. Got a suspicious death."

Now, this is not your common everyday excuse for blowing off your date, but when your lover is a detective with the Bergen County Violent Crimes Unit, you deal with it with as much grace as you can manage.

This morning, even with coffee, grace was in short supply. We'd planned to spend Saturday wandering around a crafts fair near Lincoln Center, topping the day off with dinner and jazz in the Village.

I didn't bother to hide my disappointment. "The whole weekend? How about Sunday? The fair will still be on."

Notice, though, how I'm not thrown by the words *suspicious death*. A less experienced woman might exhibit shock or fear that there could be a killer running around her normally quiet suburban neighborhood. Not me. I've learned that it's usually someone you know who does you in, or at least someone who can benefit in some way from your demise. No one except my ex could possibly benefit from mine, and I'm pretty safe on that score because having our children, a thirteen- and an eleven-year-old, living with him full-time would have a decidedly limiting effect on his lifestyle.

"Probably won't be able to get loose," Ted replied. "If I do get a break I'll try to stop by in the afternoon."

I heaved an audible sigh. "Okay."

"Don't sulk. Unless this gets completely out of hand, we'll do something next weekend. See if you can get Rich to switch his time with the kids."

"Oh, that'll work. He'll have made plans to fly to the moon or at least to the Riviera." I stood about as much chance getting Rich to give up an anticipated rendezvous as I would calling the White House and asking the President to do likewise.

"Who got whacked?" I asked in my streetwise vernacular.

"Did I say it was a homicide?"

That was his cop persona treading carefully.

"Hey, I won't rat to the press. Who was it?"

"Nobody you know, thank God. I get to catch this one all by myself."

That little dig was a not-so-subtle reference to my penchant for being in the wrong place at the wrong time, occasionally with the right motive, which too often has plunged me into extremely deep shit. Happily, Lieutenant Brodsky no longer considers me capable of murder. He knows I'm quite capable of wishing it on someone, even of devising heinous plots such as thumb-hanging or thumb-screwing, but when push comes to shove, the killer instinct just isn't there.

"She is from your neck of the woods, though," Ted went on. "Ever hear of a lady named Helena Forester?"

It rang a bell. "Isn't she the socialite from Englewood who's involved with all those charity functions?" Englewood's only a few towns away from Norwood, where, since the divorce, the kids and I now live.

"*Was* the socialite."

I swallowed. I wasn't feeling quite as flippant as I was pretending. "What happened?"

"Got run down by a bicycle. Tell you about it when I see you."

He hung up without saying more.

I placed three bowls on the counter and filled them with Cat Chow, set two on the table and filled them with raisin bran.

Got run down by a bicycle? No wonder Ted wasn't calling it a homicide. But then, why was Violent Crimes investigating? Maybe it was a hit-and-run. A hit-and-run biker. I wondered if it was one of those messenger bikes. A nineties phenomenon. If you run down a pedestrian with a bike, do they charge you as though you'd been driving a car? What if it's a juvenile riding the bike? Anyway, Ted's squad isn't usually called in on hit-and-runs. What was going on that Ted already knew he'd be tied up the entire weekend?

I've known Ted for about a year and a half, and though I'm loath to admit it even to myself (such a response being a threat to my hard-earned independence), his touch still makes my knees go weak. Besides which, I genuinely like him, maybe even—and I say this with some trepidation—maybe even love him. I think what appeals to me most is his honesty, his basic decency, traits that, after eighteen years with a womanizing shitheel, I've come to value highly. My only problem is he's beginning to mention the M word. Marriage, not murder. I realize many women of my not-so-tender years and not-so-enviable financial situation would be talking to the caterer, but it scares the hell out of me. Once burned, you know. But that's not the crux of it. It's what he does for a living. Talk about nightmares. It wouldn't take a genius to figure out the genesis of this morning's, because the one I have on a regular basis involves a couple of detectives coming to my door, faces somber, and telling me they're terribly sorry but my husband has been—well, you get the picture.

I dream a lot. I wish I didn't. But I have a checkered past.

I wish I didn't.

Take the dream I had in which I saw my much-adored then husband rolling around in the hay with his not-so-honeyish honeybun. I've tried to write that off as my subconscious e-mailing my conscious mind a wake-up call. But how do you explain the one in which I saw said honeybun floating facedown in a crimson-streaked pool of water? Okay, I admit wishful thinking played a part; the witch did deserve to be hanged by her thumbs; but the fact that both dreams turned out to have a very firm basis in reality is an uncomfortable coincidence on which I'd rather not dwell.

Take my word for it, I'm not a psychic. Sensitive to other people's vibes, yes; visual, intuitive, all prerequisites for the work I do. As a biofeedback clinician, I deal with mind–body connections. The sign on my office door reads TO CHANGE THE PRINTOUT OF THE BODY, YOU MUST LEARN TO REWRITE THE SOFTWARE OF THE MIND. That's Deepak Chopra. I teach my patients how to put themselves into an alpha state much in the way monks do, in order to bring about complete relaxation. I teach them techniques to deal with their insomnia. I can almost summon the sandman at will. For them.

When I was a teenager I dreamed romantic dreams, running off with Robert Redford or my high-school French teacher. I'd sleep like a hibernating bear through the night and wake up bright-eyed and happy as a bride the morning after. If my French teacher's still around he's probably gone gray and jowly, and Redford's appearance nowadays is a mighty rare event. Of course, I do, on occasion, have the real thing—the aforementioned sexy police lieutenant.

So far I've managed to put said lieutenant's matrimonial aspirations on hold with some relatively valid excuses: the children—they're still emotionally fragile after the divorce and the trauma of having been acquainted with murder victims; my five years of alimony, which I desperately need and which I would lose on remarriage; and the fact that we haven't known each other long enough, which doesn't hold any water at all with Ted. He's forty-five and I faced the big four-O last year, so I can't fault him when he says it's time we started living while the living's good. Particularly when you realize you can walk out your door and be done in by someone riding a bike.

I finished my coffee and placed the three Cat Chow bowls on the floor. I try to feed Luciano, Placido, and José, our Siamese cats, while Horty's outside; otherwise he'll lick their plates clean before they've had a mouthful. Horty's named after the elephant in Dr. Seuss's *Horton Hears a Who*, it being a toss-up as to which is bigger or eats more. Guess who the cats are named after?

I didn't mention my conversation with Ted to Alison and Matt while they concentrated on their cereal and toast and I prattled on about wearing ponchos and making sure to take dry socks in their backpacks. As it is, I have them both seeing a therapist, the result of the aforementioned past traumatic events. Helena Forester wasn't anyone they knew, and what had happened to her shouldn't touch them any more than the usual catastrophes they see every day on the news. I decided it shouldn't affect me personally, either, and resolutely put it out of my mind.

Not for long, though. It was all over the papers by Friday, and by Saturday someone had leaked the news that Violent Crimes was involved in the investigation. I have to confess to reading the stories with some interest. It seems Helena Forester was a prominent lady. A beauty in her youth (the picture they printed was of a brittle, upper-fortyish, attractive, carefully coiffed and made-up woman), she was extremely wealthy and well known for her business smarts and her philanthropy. According to the papers, she had established her own charitable foundation with the profits from a successful travel business, was active in support of the arts, and had received numerous commendations for her generosity. She'd been married twice, the first to a wealthy widower with a young daughter. He'd expired several years later, and a few years ago she'd married a high-school teacher from Tenafly by the name of Andrew Klinger. Before and in between there had been numerous "liaisons," one with the late (and very married) prominent Wall Street financier Chandler Harrington, and one with the popular soap opera actor Brad Weber. But the most notable was a longtime affair with a lawyer by the name of Donald Grasso, a name that today has become a household word as a result of a couple of media-circus trials. I'd watched him on *Geraldo* Friday night looking somber but exuding the enormous charm that had catapulted him to national prominence, extolling the virtues of his ex-lover. Which made me wonder why she was an ex. I can't imagine Rich making a nice speech about me, but I'm an ex-*wife*. Then again, maybe if I were dead—well, I'll never know. The high-school teacher was, I thought, kind of an odd finale to such an illustrious list of high rollers. Neither marriage had resulted in children. Helena, who had kept her maiden name, had been born in Queens, New York, in 1950. Very little was known of her childhood. As an adult she'd lived in New York City, briefly in Beverly Hills, ultimately in Englewood, New Jersey, and over the years had done a good deal of traveling, mostly connected with her business. I always think, when I read about someone who's crammed so much activity into her time on earth, that I'm lacking something. I mean, if I bought it in an airplane crash tomorrow, how would my obituary read? *Caroline Carlin, biofeedback clinician, born 1958, graduated from Cornell University, married, divorced, leaves two wonderful children, four animals, died 1999 having done nothing memorable.* At times like these, a little voice in my head says, *"Take some risks, Carrie. Marry Ted. Or at least get out there and save the whales."*

The only details given in the paper on Friday about the circumstances of Ms. Forester's death were that the police were searching for the biker who had sped off. No mention of the death being suspicious. But on Saturday they announced that there had been a witness. No name, but the scuttlebutt had it that the witness said the biker had knocked Helena Forester down with malice aforethought. Aha. The reason for Ted's "suspicious death."

Ted never made it over on the weekend, and I spoke to him only once, very briefly. He was on the run, and I know him well enough to know when not to press. I didn't bring up the case. I just had time to tell him that, as expected, Rich had unbreakable plans for next weekend—a jaunt to the Bahamas, not the moon.

Rich had picked up the kids at nine on Saturday, and I'd left for my office right after they did. I usually do only brain-wave training with my Attention Deficit Disorder (ADD) kids on Saturday mornings, but today I had three ADDs and one Stress Management. I was surprised that none of the mothers mentioned the incident when I went out to talk to them after each child's session, but I guess that's because my office is in Piermont, which, while only two towns away from Norwood, is in New York State. Someone being knocked down by a bike, even with malice, just isn't front-page news in New York. What did bring Helena Forester to mind again was the call I received from Jenny Margolies, canceling her session. She told me she was canceling so she could attend the funeral.

"Oh, Jenny, I'm sorry," I said. "I didn't realize you knew her."

"Yes," Jenny said tightly, "I knew her."

"Terrible what happened. She must've been a wonderful woman. According to the papers, she——"

"I don't think *wonderful* is exactly the word I'd use," Jenny interrupted. "I'm not going to the funeral to weep over her. I plan to dance on her grave."

I repeated the remark to my best friend, Meg Reilly, when I dropped by her café, which is just down the street from my office, for lunch. Meg's Place is where I come whenever I'm feeling gloomy. Also when I'm not gloomy, just hungry. I can feed my stomach and my soul at the same time at the same watering trough. Aside from the fact that Meg herself is a tonic for me, just walking in the door lifts my spirits. No matter the time of year, colorful spring-flower arrangements burst from the huge antique vases that Meg takes on consignment from Golden Oldies, the antique shop down the street. The walls are overlaid with her unique photographs, although there are no longer, as there used to be, any of her husband, Kevin, and his brother, Pete, grinning audaciously from the deck of their sleek blue-and-silver-striped powerboat. Pete was killed at the offshore powerboat races in Key West last year. I thought Kev would give up racing, but he's going back again this year, exactly as Ted had prophesied. I don't know how Meg stands it, but it's not my business. Who am I to talk anyway? I'm with a cop. Maybe the problem lies with Meg and me. What attracts us to the adventurers?

"Wasn't that a weird thing for Jenny to say?" I commented. "If you believe the papers, the woman was a cross between Audrey Hepburn and Princess Di."

Meg pulled up a chair and sat down across from me. "Well, things aren't always what they seem."

The piece of quiche on my fork didn't make it to my mouth. "What do you mean?"

She looked uncomfortable, gave a quick glance around, then leaned forward and whispered in my ear. "I don't know if I should tell you this. . . ."

Meg and I have been through the wars together. There's almost nothing we don't tell each other. I raised my eyebrows, pretended to be insulted. "You can't tell me something about a perfect stranger?"

"It involves someone else. Someone you know. In a way I'd be betraying a confidence."

Now, I would like to say that I immediately dropped the subject, not wanting to put my best friend in an untenable position, but that's not the way it went. She'd brought it up and my curiosity was aroused. "Ted's department's involved, you know," I remarked loftily. "I'll find out."

Meg chuckled. "Yeah, like he keeps you apprised of everything that's happening in an ongoing investigation."

She knew whereof she spoke. Ted could be very closemouthed when it came to his work. "Come on, Meg. You know I'm the soul of discretion."

"This doesn't go any further. You swear?"

"Swear."

"It's Franny."

"Franny? Franny of Golden Oldies? What's she got to do with it?" Franny Gold is one of the gentlest, sweetest people I've ever known. Of indeterminate age, somewhere between seventy and eighty plus, she's a throwback to a time when manners were the order of the day and the word *damn*, much less *shit*, never passed a lady's lips. She dresses straight out of the last century and serves you tea out of delicate china cups, also out of the last century. An antique shop is the perfect environment for Franny. I've never heard her raise her voice in all the years I've been going to her shop, which is just three doors down from my office. I often stop by Golden Oldies to chat and browse on my way home, and I always come away feeling as though the world is a better place than I'd thought it was when I went in.

"She came in Saturday morning totally freaked out. I've never seen her like that. It took three cups of chamomile to calm her down."

Meg employs chamomile tea the way other people do Valium. She'd plied me with many a cup in the early days of our friendship when I was going through my divorce. "So, what was it?"

Meg lowered her voice. "Franny's the witness the papers are talking about. She saw it happen."

I drew in my breath. "Oh, my God, poor Franny. No wonder she's shook up."

"That's not the whole thing. She said Helena was coming out of the John Harms theater just as she, Franny, was crossing the street. Franny knows her from the shop. She was there with another lady just a few weeks ago and she owed Franny quite a bit of money for something she'd bought, so when—"

"She knew her? That has to make it—"

"Will you shut up and listen? You know Van Brunt's a fairly quiet street. There weren't many people around. She said the guy on the bike came around the corner from Palisade Avenue riding on the sidewalk. When he saw Helena he picked up speed and headed straight for her. He was waving something that looked to Franny kind of like a lasso. Whatever it was caught Helena on the side of the head. Franny said the woman dropped like a stone and the guy took off. It wasn't the bike that knocked her down, like the papers said. And it definitely wasn't an accident."

2

＊

I KNEW TED or someone from his department had probably already interviewed Franny. I was
dying to talk to him about it, but by Monday he still
hadn't called. Franny's shop was closed over the weekend, which to my knowledge was the first time ever in
twenty years. Wednesdays through Sundays are her big-
gest days, especially the weekends, when the tourists
descend in droves on Piermont. I rang her bell on my
way to my office, but there was no answer.

Jenny Margolies had rescheduled for Monday afternoon, and I have to admit I was looking forward to her
session with a little more than my usual enthusiasm. I
was beginning to see what fascinated Ted about this
business. If you weren't personally connected to any of
the people involved and you could put aside your aversion to dead bodies—pleasanter, of course, when you
don't have to view them all bloody and revoltingly

smelly—the puzzle-solving aspect of a murder can be intriguing. Why do people kill? It's a subject about which I've come to have some understanding—and a little not-so-welcome experience. And if you stretch your imagination, you can find a connection between what Ted does and what I do. We both deal with the human mind with all its devious twists and turns. Admittedly, I focus more on the spiritual while Ted deals with the darker side, but over the years I've had a few off-the-wallers myself.

Jenny isn't one of them. I've been seeing her twice a week for four months for stress management since she lost her job. She'd been working for one of the big ad agencies and had seemed to be successfully climbing the ladder when six months ago she got caught in a downsizing squeeze. She's temporarily moved back home with her parents, a bad idea, I think, because till now she hasn't been looking very hard for a new job and has been really down in the mouth.

Jenny is your typical New York yuppie. She's twenty-six, has thick brown hair that falls in waves to her shoulders, green eyes, freckles, perfect all-American features, an excellent education to go with her good brain, lots of ambition, and more than a smattering of the arrogance that comes with having taken those attributes for granted all her life. Today she was wearing a snappy little Ann Taylor navy blue suit and a rose silk blouse that complemented the color in her cheeks.

"You look like you're on your way somewhere," I said as I reached for the leads. "Dare I ask if it's a job interview?"

She grinned. "You could and it is."

"Terrific. What happened?"

"A great impediment to my getting work has been miraculously removed."

"How's that?" I inquired as I attached the sensors to her fingers.

"Never mind," she trilled. "But I think you're going to see a big drop in my EDR."

EDR is electrodermal response or, in lay terms, internal tension level, the old fight-or-flight response. I glanced at the monitor. A three. The lowest I'd managed to get her at her last session was a twelve. "Well, well, I wish I could take credit, but you seem to be doing this all on your own."

"Oh, you've helped, but the rest was God's doing." She laughed. "Well, not entirely. God had a little assist."

That did it. I had to know. "Could this have anything to do with the funeral you just attended?"

She giggled again. "It could."

This was getting interesting. "Jenny, what's your connection to Helena Forester?"

"None now, thank God."

"Why'd you go to the funeral?"

"To make sure she was really dead. I even went to the cemetery just to watch them plant her."

She said it with such glee that a shiver ran through me, because I'm a little (*just* a little) ashamed to tell you I could relate to her delight. I remembered how I'd felt when I first learned about the death of Erica Vogel, Rich's intended. Horror mixed with shock mixed with—dare I admit it?—satisfaction that the bitch from hell got her just desserts. I glanced back at the monitor. Jenny's EDR had risen several microhms. I decided I shouldn't be feeding into this. My job, after all, is to lower tension level, not raise it.

"Okay, enough chitchat. Let's get to work. We want you in good shape for the interview. Who's it with, by the way?"

"Saatchi and Saatchi."

"Good for you. We'll do some positive affirmations for self-esteem." I walked behind her, lowered the chair to a reclining position, and turned down the light. Then I pushed the PLAY button on my tape recorder and allowed the soft music to fill the room. "Close your eyes and take a deep, deep breath," I intoned. "Allow yourself to imagine or sense a warm, healing light flowing down—"

"You should've heard the kudos, though," Jenny interrupted, her eyes wide open. "The eulogies. My God, you'd've thought they were burying Joan of Arc."

Hardly an apt analogy since poor Joan was burned at the stake and, I'm pretty sure, *sans* eulogies.

"Well," I began tentatively, "according to what I've read, she did seem to have earned at least some of—"

"Earned?" Jenny sat bolt upright, pulling loose the sensor I'd just attached to her trapezius. "She earned shit. Everything she ever had, she stole!"

"Relax, Jenny," I said, carefully reattaching the sensor as I watched her EDR soar. "The woman's dead. She can't steal from you or anyone anymore."

Jenny leaned back and closed her eyes. "No, but what's done can't be undone."

"Shakespeare, right?" I said, trying to lighten the mood. "Who said that?"

"Lady MacBeth, who couldn't get the blood off her hands."

My stomach did one of those crazy flip-flops like when an elevator drops suddenly. "Did Helena Forester have blood on her hands?"

Jenny didn't answer right away. Then she opened her eyes and sat up, "I knew Laurel, her first husband's daughter. Laurel's parents and mine were good friends."

There was a long pause.

"Yes, so. . . ?"

"I used to envy Laurel. Her mother—her name was Juliana—she was Eurasian and beautiful like her name. I was only ten when she died, but I'll never forget her. Laurel was thirteen."

I felt a chill. My Allie is thirteen. It's such a critical time in a young girl's development, a time when she really needs her mother. "What was it?" I asked. "Cancer?"

She hesitated. "They said suicide."

I caught my breath—couldn't help an involuntary shudder. "What happened?"

"She used to get these cluster headaches. Violently painful. She had medication for them. One night she overdosed."

"How awful. On purpose, do you think?"

"I doubt it. When she wasn't having those headaches, she was very happy. She adored Laurel and Lyle, Laurel's dad. Anyone who knew them feels she would never have done anything like that deliberately."

The silence lay heavy like a cloud about to burst.

"So it was accidental suicide."

"Laurel's father was out of town on business that day. When the pain got so bad Juliana knew she'd have to take medication that would knock her out, she called up a friend and asked her to come over so Laurel would have an adult in the house." Jenny began rubbing her temples with her free hand as if she herself had a headache. "Laurel found her mother on the bathroom floor the next morning. She'd gone to her room before leaving for school to see how Juliana was doing. The pill bottle was next to her, empty."

I hesitated, not sure where she was going with this. "It's a terrible story, Jenny, but I don't see the connection."

"Helena Forester was the friend. Actually she'd been the family travel agent, who'd sort of insinuated herself into the family over the years. She said she gave Juliana two pain pills, stayed with her till she fell asleep, then went downstairs to the guest room. But Laurel's room was right next to her mother's and she said she heard voices, a man's and a woman's, in her mother's room around three in the morning. When she knocked on the door, Helena said the doctor was with her mother, but that everything was all right and she should go back to sleep."

It took a few seconds for the implication to become clear. "Are you saying—oh, come on, Jenny. Just because you and she had a thing—"

"Helena swore Laurel had dreamed the whole thing. Nobody believed her, not even her dad. Everyone thought she was in shock and grieving so terribly she needed someone to blame."

"Well, you can understand—I mean, why would—"

"Helena and Laurel's father were married a year later. He was nineteen years older than she was and very wealthy."

"How could she have known he'd—how could she plan that?"

Jenny lay back, began taking the deep diaphragmatic breaths I'd taught her. "You ever see the musical *Damn Yankees?*"

"Yeah, quite a while ago. Why?"

"There's a song in it." She sang the first bar. *"Whatever Lola wants, Lola gets."*

"Okay, I get it. But if I remember correctly, Lola was a witch."

"So was Helena. And if you think Cinderella had it tough," she added, closing her eyes, "you should talk to Laurel sometime."

After a minute I glanced at the monitor. Her EDR was back to three. Mine, I'm absolutely certain, was not. I continued with the exercise, but my mind was whirling like one of those dreidels my assistant, Ruth-Ann, gives my kids at Hanukkah.

When Jenny was putting on her coat, I wished her luck with the interview and set up a session for Thursday. I knew I was treading on thin ice, but I had to say it. "Whatever the truth is about what happened to your friend all those years ago, Jenny, it's over. You should encourage her to see a therapist. She's got a lot to work out."

Jenny laughed. "You don't know the half of it." At the door she turned. "Aren't you seeing that detective who was at the funeral?"

How'd she know that? "What'd he look like?"

"Tall, thin, forties, kind of attractive in an offbeat sort of way."

"Sounds like him." The papers hadn't called Helena's death a homicide, but Jenny's remark that God had an assist meant she knew something that the press didn't. Yet. "I didn't know he'd gone to the funeral," I said.

"I heard he's a homicide dick. I don't want him questioning me because of what I told you today."

"I consider what you tell me in this office privileged,

but what would he question you about?" I asked, feigning innocence. "The woman was knocked down by a guy on a bike. It was probably an accident."

"That's not what people at the funeral were saying."

"What were they saying?"

"That she was hit on the head. The bike never touched her."

That certainly jibed with what Franny said she saw. "Wow," I murmured. "Who said that?"

"Her husband, for one. That asshole teacher. And he must know. He ID'd the body."

After she'd gone, I realized she'd never said if she had a personal beef with Helena Forester or if her dislike was all based on the experience of her friend.

"It's consistent with what Franny told you," I said to Meg when I stopped by the café on my way home.

Meg continued filling the nut dishes and placing them next to the bud vases on each table. "It does sound like what she described. Has Ted said anything?"

"I haven't spoken to him. If he hasn't called he must be working sixteen hours a day."

Meg grinned. "Pretty sure of him, aren't you?"

I shrugged. "For the moment."

"Oh, Carrie, why that man puts up with you! You give him such a hard time."

"Not true. I give him a very good time. I'm just not in the marriage market."

Meg shook her head. "Opportunity's knocking and you're screwing up."

I popped a nut into my mouth. "Why is marriage the

only way to go? Just because it works for you and Kevin doesn't mean it's for everyone."

"It isn't the only way. But Ted wants a commitment from you and you're still making him pay for Rich. You could lose him, Carrie."

Bad enough I have to dance around Ted every time he brings up the subject, I thought grumpily. *Now my best friend's on my case.* "Can we get back to our original discussion? What do you say we go talk to Franny? If she's sitting in that apartment all alone she must be a basket case by now. She needs her friends."

Meg gave me a quizzical glance. "You sure that's your only motive? I think this crime-solving stuff is beginning to get in your blood."

"You're the one who wants me to marry Rambo."

She threw up her hands. "I give up. Just let me get my coat."

She headed for the kitchen and I reached for my jacket. "She didn't open this weekend, you know," I called after her.

"I know. She's not answering the phone either." Meg appeared in the doorway followed by a skinny young woman with frizzy brown hair and a spotted complexion, wearing a white shirt and dark pants. "Betsy, will you be okay for an hour or so?" she asked her. "It'll be slow tonight."

"No problem," the girl responded.

"If Mr. Reilly stops in, give him the goulash and tell him I'll join him later."

"Okay."

A blast of cold air made me draw my jacket close around me as the door closed behind us. "Where'd she come from?" I inquired.

"I just started her. She's coming in part-time. I needed someone now that it looks like Franny's out of commission."

Franny used to help Meg out in the café on her off days.

"I'd gotten so I depended on Franny so that Kev and I could have a few free evenings a week."

"Is it okay to leave a new girl alone like that?"

"Well, I'll find out, won't I? She seems pretty together and she had good references. Apparently she hasn't got much of a social life. Doesn't mind working Saturday nights. Franny may not be able to cover me for quite a while. She might even have left town."

"I'm sure Ted warned her not to go anywhere," I answered. "If she's the only witness, they're going to want her to be available."

Meg grimaced. "How could I forget that?" Meg was the only witness to the accident that killed her brother-in-law just last winter, although at the time she wasn't aware that she'd seen anything significant. To say the police were inflexible when we wanted to leave Key West before the investigation was concluded is putting it mildly.

The Christmas lights were already replacing the leaves on the branches, a cheerful sight as we walked toward Franny's shop. It wasn't even turkey time, but in Piermont there were little candelabra lights on every tree along the main street—just one of the things I love about the place. I chose to have my office here because the town manages to combine old-world charm with crass commercialism and make it work. The main street is just a few blocks long, but there are enough shops and restaurants to attract customers, even in the evening. I never feel lonely in Piermont.

Franny lives in a little apartment above her store. As I glanced up I could see the shades were drawn. It was difficult to tell whether or not the lights were on. Meg rang the bell. There was no answer.

"Keep ringing," I said. "She's got to be there."

"Maybe she's gone to a friend's or a relative's," Meg said. "Does she have any family?"

"You know," I replied, feeling slightly ashamed, "I never asked her. She's been kind of a fixture here ever since I've been coming to this town. She never talks about family, and I never thought to ask." I looked up and thought I detected a tiny sliver of light peeking through the shade. "Franny," I called. "It's Carrie and Meg. Can we come up?"

The shade moved again, then fell back into place, and a minute later I heard footsteps on the stairs. The door opened halfway.

"Come in," Franny whispered. "Hurry."

She looked distraught, disheveled, totally out of character. Her gray hair had come loose from its knot, wisps hanging in her face and down her back. She was wearing a faded robe of a kind of indiscriminate pinkish-purple color and floppy slippers on her feet that clattered as she walked ahead of us up the steps. Meg and I exchanged glances. We'd never seen Franny attired in anything other than one of her elegant nineteenth-century lacy dresses and sensible shoes.

The room she led us to was dark. Only one lamp, which looked like a real Tiffany to my admittedly amateur eyes, was lit. The light sifted through the vivid reds and greens and golds of the glass, throwing kaleidoscopic shadows, lending an eerie sense of movement to the large bronze eagle sitting in the center of the mantelpiece. It gave me the creeps. I perched gingerly on the edge of a delicately carved wood chair, fearful my hundred and twelve pounds might cause it to disintegrate under me. Meg sat on the burgundy velvet love seat opposite. Franny stood between us, wringing her hands, then burst into tears.

Meg pulled her down beside her. "It's okay, it's okay," she murmured soothingly. "There's no reason to be so upset."

"There is," Franny sobbed.

"Of course she's upset," I said. "It must've been horrendous, seeing that."

"It was," Franny sobbed, "but that's not it."

I was at a loss. "Then what—"

"The papers, they said there was a witness."

"So what? No one knows it was you."

"I only got a quick look," she sobbed. "It all happened so fast. The police kept asking me questions and I had to look at hundreds of pictures in books, but I told them I didn't see him up close. I didn't think I'd be able to identify him."

"Well, then, what's the problem?" Meg asked.

"He thinks I can."

"Franny, you're being paranoid. Your name wasn't mentioned. How could anyone—"

"Someone," she hiccuped, her eyes wild, "someone stuck a . . . something through my mail slot Saturday night."

"What kind of something?"

She got up and clomped into the bedroom, returning a minute later with a covered shoe box. "This," she whispered hoarsely, handing me the box. "The thing in the box."

I removed the cover gingerly, half-expecting it to blow up in my face.

"Don't touch it," Meg said. "There might be fingerprints."

I threw her an "as if I wouldn't know that after all my crime-fighting experience" look. We both peered at the object lying on the bottom of the box.

"What is it?" I asked.

Meg shrugged. "Damned if I know. Maybe it's an antique someone wants you to sell for them," she said to Franny.

"People don't slide valuable antiques through the mail slot of my shop."

She had a point. Speaking of points, it had four. I'd never seen anything like it. It was kind of star-shaped, a dull battleship-gray color less than an eighth of an inch thick with jagged edges that looked frighteningly lethal. Something had been scratched into the surface, the outline of a monkey or a chimp. I couldn't tell exactly how heavy it was without picking it up, but it seemed to have weight.

"What makes you think this has anything to do with what you saw?" I asked.

"The monkey has its paws over its mouth. Someone's telling me to keep quiet or I'll end up dead like Helena."

I rolled my eyes in disbelief at Meg, then we both looked at the star again. The outline was faint, but from a certain angle there did seem to be paws covering the mouth. Maybe Franny hadn't totally lost it. Maybe she really was in trouble.

Tears welled up and ran in rivulets down the creases

in her cheeks. "Why won't you believe me? I'm not crazy."

"No one's saying you are," I replied, patting her hand. "Why don't we call the police and see what they think?"

"No! He's probably watching the house."

"Oh, Franny," Meg said. "If Helena really was murdered, the killer is long gone."

"I'll call Ted," I said. "No point in bringing in the local cops anyway. It's his case. I'll tell him to come alone and bring a bottle of wine. If the house is being watched, it'll look like we're all here for dinner."

I didn't wait for Franny to find the holes in my logic. I picked up the phone, which was on an end table wedged between an old metal bank that looked like a jukebox and a china-doll head that had misplaced its body. The doll head gave me the creeps worse than the eagle. I punched in the number of the precinct in Hackensack, hoping Ted would still be there. He was. I told him Meg and I were with Franny and that I thought it was important he come right away—she had something he should see. He picked up on the urgency in my voice and didn't argue.

"On my way," he said and hung up.

After that, I called home and told Allie I was delayed —she should warm up the lasagna in the fridge.

"Tell Matt to walk Horty and then feed him and the cats while you make a salad," I instructed. "If I'm not home in an hour, you guys go ahead and eat, and no TV till you've done your homework."

"I knooow," she drawled. "Where are you, Mom?"

"At Franny's. She's not feeling well." With no further explanation, I gave her the number and hung up.

Ted arrived in less than an hour—as instructed, carrying an unbagged bottle of wine. I hoped it was a decent one. Shades of my past, by now I'd welcome a drink. Meg and I had combed Franny's hair and made her change into a dress. She was looking slightly less like a crazed homeless person by the time the doorbell rang, although she jumped at the sound.

"Relax, Franny. It's Ted," I said. "He's not going to bite your head off. Just tell him what's happened."

When I opened the door, Ted grinned at me and shook his head in mock incredulity. "What is it about you?"

"Well, that's a lovely greeting," I replied. "You sound like Eve."

Eve's my father's relatively new wife. In her eyes I'm the reason for my father's heart attack plus every minor pain in the neck or any other part of his anatomy he's had ever since.

"And after we may have found your murder weapon for you too," I added indignantly.

The brows furrowed. "Show me." He walked in, taking in the room at a glance. Meg had found the light switch for the overhead chandelier, and I suddenly became aware of my surroundings. A patterned magenta Persian rug blanketed the floor. Wherever the eye lit there were objects: vases of every shape and color, figurines, apothecary bottles, old shaving mugs, all lined up on the mantel, on the end tables, on the mahogany pie-crust table on which the Tiffany lamp stood, on every available surface, even on the dark oak floor bordering the rug. The velvet love seat wore old hand-crocheted lace antimacassars on its arms. Every inch of space on the wall was covered with pictures—pictures of Early American flat-faced men in wigs, women in bonnets,

Hudson River scenes. Oriental landscapes painted on glass were hung beside samurai warriors water-colored on parchment. Here was Franny's inventory, each piece a treasure, I was sure. But the clutter combined with the mustiness permeating the air made me feel suddenly uneasy, as though I'd been transported to a time and place where I was surrounded by ghosts. I knew my reaction was silly—undoubtedly based on my aversion to dusting—and I tried to shake it off.

Ted was already examining the star. He'd donned rubber gloves and was turning it over in his hand.

"Not the murder weapon," he said. "The Forester woman was killed by a blow to the head. This or anything similar would have been embedded in her skull."

"How do you know she didn't strike her head when she fell?" I asked. "Maybe it really was an accident."

Ted looked at Franny. "Our witness says different," he said. "Right, Franny?"

She nodded. "He was waving something in the air, like he was going to rope a cow. It hit her."

"Maybe it scared her and made her fall," I hypothesized, "and she hit her head on the curb." I turned to Ted. "Isn't that possible?"

"It'll depend on what the M.E. says about the angle of the wound as opposed to how she was lying. Either way the perpetrator would still be responsible."

"But it would've been involuntary manslaughter," I went on, trying to make my point. "And the person wouldn't be interested in making his situation worse by coming after Franny." I sat down on the love seat, pleased with my assessment.

Ted didn't answer, but I could tell he wasn't buying

the involuntary part. Neither was Franny. She was rocking back and forth and hugging herself.

"What was he doing waving that thing in the first place, and why did he slide this awful star thing under my door?"

Why indeed? I looked at Ted, waiting for him to come up with something to ease Franny's mind.

"It's possible the incidents aren't related," he said carefully.

"There, you see?" I said to Franny. "Tomorrow somebody'll probably call and tell you they wanted your opinion on the age of the—"

"Still," Ted interrupted, "I think it would be a very good idea if you closed your shop and stayed with a friend for the time being. No point in asking for trouble."

So much for my efforts. I eyed the wine longingly.

3
*

GUESS WHO the friend turned out to be? Franny came home with me. Meg went back to the café and Ted followed my car to my house. He came in, so I fed both him and Franny what was left of the lasagna. Lasagna doesn't last very long around my kids, but there was plenty of salad, and fortunately, only Ted was hungry. Franny barely managed three bites and I concentrated on the wine he'd brought, which was a very drinkable California merlot. Talk was minimal, confined to where Franny would sleep. I finally decided to bring Allie in with me for what I hoped would be only a couple of nights.

While Ted cleared the table, I took Franny upstairs and got her settled in Allie's room and Allie in mine. Then I came back to the kitchen. Ted had loaded the dishwasher and was vigorously scrubbing the counter.

"Want a job?" I asked teasingly. "I could use a house-keeper."

"What're you offering?"

"Well, let's see. How's five bucks a day and love on demand?"

"I'll take it. When do I move in?" he rejoined, slipping his arms around my waist.

I'd certainly set myself up for that one. "Your hands are wet." I moved out of his grasp and tossed him a towel. I don't know why I did it, and instantly I regretted it. A shutter came down over his eyes. He picked up his jacket.

"Ted, I'm sorry," I said. "I guess I'm just nervous about all this. Could we talk about what's going on with Franny?"

His voice was cool. "Nothing to talk about. Pending autopsy results, Forester's death is classified only as suspicious." He headed for the door.

"Don't leave like this. I said I was sorry."

He paused, his hand on the doorknob. He didn't look at me. "You don't have to apologize for your feelings."

"That's not it. I didn't mean—"

He held up his hand. "We want different things. I'm making you uncomfortable pressuring you. But that's over. You can stop worrying about it. As far as the investigation goes, it's not your affair."

What did he mean, *"that's over"*? "But I want to help," I mumbled.

"Just keep your eye on Franny till we pick up the biker. There's nothing else for you to do. Say 'bye to the kids for me." He reached down and stroked Horty, who was licking his hand, and then he was gone.

"Say 'bye to the kids?" What did *that* mean? *"You could lose*

him, Carrie." Meg's words resounded in my head. What was wrong with me? I couldn't explain my reaction even to myself. Did I want to lose Ted? If I did, I was certainly doing all the right things, and hurting him in the bargain. A memory came back to me, so vivid I felt almost physically sick. Rich in his favorite chair, reading. I'd gone over and sat on his lap, and he'd jumped up so quickly, I'd fallen on the floor. He'd apologized, of course, told me I'd taken him by surprise, but the message was clear. Keep off. I remembered refusing his hand as I struggled to my feet, the pain in my heart greater than the one in my back. I didn't want to do that to Ted, but hadn't I just made him feel the same way? Was I getting even? Had I become one of those embittered women who unconsciously make every man suffer for what one man did? Or was it all pure cowardice, fear of getting involved for fear of getting hurt again? I felt miserable. I gave it nearly an hour and called his apartment in Hackensack. It rang four times and his machine picked up.

"Ted, are you there?" I waited several seconds and then went on, my voice hesitant. "I don't know what's wrong with me . . . but . . . I know I care for you and the last thing I want to do is hurt you. Could you be a little patient while I try to work things out?" I waited, not knowing what else to say, and was about to hang up when he picked up.

"I'm getting old and gray. How long do you expect this working-out process to take?"

Considering the way I'd been acting, the enormous sense of relief I felt would be enough to give Freud, much less my old therapist, a headache. "Suppose we say by your forty-sixth birthday?"

"Okay, you got three months."

Damn, why hadn't I said *my* forty-sixth?

"You'd better make an appointment with your shrink," he added, uncannily reading my mind.

I was about to make a snappy rejoinder when I heard footsteps clattering on the stairs. I looked up and saw Franny, wearing her fuzzy purplish robe, standing in the doorway.

"I know why I connected the star with the man on the bicycle," she whispered.

"Ted, hold on a minute," I said. "Franny's remembered something." I turned to her. "Why, Franny?"

"There was a kind of star on the back of his hand, a large tattoo, I think. He rode right by me before he—he speeded up and his hand was right out there on the handlebar grip. The tattoo was black and a different shape than the star in the box, rounder in the middle with lots of odd-shaped spikes coming out, but the more I think about it, it was a star."

"Ted, did you hear?"

"Yeah." There was a pause on the other end of the line. "Carrie?"

"Yes?"

"Don't repeat this, but I don't want Franny left alone. Take her to the office with you tomorrow."

"Okay. Why?"

"The star with the oddly shaped spikes she's describing—it reminds me—I just don't like the sound of it. I'm not sure what the connection is to Helena Forester, but I'm damned well going to find out."

* * *

It was another one of those nights. I couldn't get Ted's words out of my mind. He's not an alarmist, although I have accused him of being overprotective where I'm concerned. What did he mean—he didn't like the sound of it? Was the star some kind of cult symbol? He wouldn't elaborate, but it was apparent he thought Franny could be in real danger. Worse, no one had any idea where it was coming from. I resolved that tomorrow I'd ask Ruth-Ann where she got her pepper spray. Ruth-Ann, who's now my afternoon assistant, is a former patient who'd been a rape victim. An Orthodox Jew, she once said to me, "Never again," and she carried her ounce of prevention to make sure.

I tossed and turned. I thought about Jenny, wondered again what Helena Forester had done to her to bring about such animosity. Jenny was so young. I was almost forty before I'd gotten to the point of actually wishing someone dead. Did Jenny know more about Helena's death than she'd told me in our session? And what about the daughter whose mother had killed herself? I wondered if Ted knew about Laurel. Where was she now, and what was the rest of that story? I was honor-bound not to reveal anything that Jenny had told me in confidence, but what if the information were crucial to the case? Ethically, what would be the right thing to do? It was a question I'd never been forced to consider before. Maybe I could get Jenny to set up a meeting for me with the daughter, see how I felt after I talked with her. It seemed clear to me that she was a young woman who needed help. I tossed some more. Who, I wondered, was the other woman with Helena in Franny's shop? I'd forgotten to ask Franny if she knew her. For sure, Ted and his squad were out looking for her.

I thought again about Helena. She was rich, and there was the side of her depicted by her lawyer friend, Grasso, who'd extolled her to the skies on national TV, and by the coworkers from the charitable foundation. If she were as bad as Jenny said, how come some people were saying such nice things about her? It couldn't just be that old reluctance to speak ill of the dead. I speak ill of dead Erica Vogel without a worry in the world that I'll be struck by lightning. It could be money. After all, assuming she'd left a chunk to the foundation, it'd look pretty crummy to bad-mouth your benefactor as she lay in her coffin. Or maybe they were afraid they'd be suspect if they told the truth about their feelings. And what was the story with the husband, Klinger? Now, there was a man with a motive. With or without a will, even if there'd been a prenup, I think he'd inherit a third of Helena's estate. He could say good-bye to those hyperactive teenagers forever. Maybe it was the husband riding that bike last week.

I jostled Horty and he growled in his sleep. Allie shifted position, her knees making what felt like permanent indentations in my back. I moved to the edge of the bed and nearly fell off. You try sleeping in a bed—even a queen-size one—with a thirteen-year-old who's already taller than you are, a duo or trio of cats depending on when you last checked, and a hundred-plus-pound dog. In the end I took my squishy pillow and a blanket, staggered downstairs, and curled up on the couch in the family room, where I finally fell into a restless sleep.

In my dreams Ted was tossing metal stars like Frisbees and Horty was chasing them. Every time he caught one, it cut his mouth and he bled. I was running back and forth between the two trying to catch the stars before

Horty got them, but I was too slow. And Ted was laughing, and then finally I caught one and in a fury tossed it back at him. And I saw it slice into the back of his jacket. And the jacket had a black star emblem on it. And it wasn't Ted. And the star began bleeding.

I woke up, sweating.

4

✦

"HOW LONG'S FRANNY going to be stay-
ing here, Mom?" Allie asked the next morning as she
pulled on her tights.

"I'm not sure, honey, but we'll move as much of your
stuff in here as you'll need for a few days. I'll clear out a
couple of drawers and make some room in the closet." I
gave her a quick hug. "Appreciate your not making a
fuss."

She ran my hairbrush through her curly black hair. "I
don't mind. Is she having her place painted or something?"

I hesitated. I don't like lies. I used to be really terrible
at them myself, couldn't fool my cats, but Meg tells me
I've improved. I'm pretty sure she doesn't mean it as a
compliment. In this case I fudged, which is what people
who have guilt about lying call it when they don't tell
the whole truth. "No. She's had an upsetting experience,

38

and Meg and I thought she'd feel better being with friends."

Happily, Allie didn't pursue it. She had something else on her mind.

"I'm thinking of trying out for the community theater production this year."

"Sounds like fun. What's the show?"

"The Mikado."

"Gilbert and Sullivan. Right up your alley." Allie has a wonderful soprano voice, honed to perfection—in my eyes, at least—by several years of expensive voice lessons. "You're in like Flynn, sweetheart."

"I'm sure I'll only get a small part if I get anything at all. I think I might have a chance for one of the little maids."

"Go for it, baby."

She grinned, planted a kiss on my cheek, and humming some lilting Gilbert-and-Sullivanish thing, took off down the stairs. I stood, listening, swelling with parental pride as though I, not God, had given her this gift.

"If that director doesn't cast her," I told my reflection in the mirror, "he is a stupid, talentless drone!"

In an effort to get her mind off her troubles, I mentioned the conversation to Franny as we drove to my office.

"The Mikado," Franny said, displaying the first glimmer of interest she'd shown in anything all morning. "That's a wonderful operetta. I wonder if they could use any help with the props or costumes."

"I should think they'd jump at it, Franny," I said, thrilled with my success.

"I have all kinds of oriental things. They'd have to be careful with them, of course. They're antiques, like me."

"Come on, you're no antique. You're just a little depressed right now. This'll be great for you. I'll ask Allie to talk to the director. I'll bet they're going to need all kinds of stuff, fans and hats and—um . . . parasols . . ." It'd been on the tip of my tongue to say *swords*, but I swallowed the word. I didn't want to mention weapons of any sort.

"Maybe you could drop me at my shop and I'll look around."

I fudged again. "I'd love to look around with you. Why don't you wait for me at Meg's Place? You can have tea and one of Meg's delicious muffins, and I'll meet you at lunchtime. We'll take a run over to the shop together."

She saw right through me. "You can't be my guard dog, Carrie. It's very sweet of you, but I'm going to have to get over this and open my shop. I'm losing business."

"Tuesdays are always slow for you. Why don't you at least wait till the weekend? Let's see what Ted comes up with by then."

We passed the pond and crossed the little bridge by the Baptist church and drove down the main street in Piermont. I began searching for a parking space, always a hassle on a main thoroughfare meant for horses and buggies. "By the way," I said casually. "I've been meaning to ask you. Any idea who the woman who came in your shop with Helena was?"

"No. Until they had the argument I thought she was probably with the foundation. The Forester woman had been in before. A few months ago she came in with Marlene Beasley and I donated a picture—"

"What argument?"

"Didn't I tell you about that?"

"No. Did you tell Ted?"

"I'm sure I did. It wasn't a big thing. I didn't hear what it was about, but Helena was looking at a piece of jewelry and the woman said something I didn't hear and then Helena laughed—not a nice laugh, really. Rather a nasty laugh. And then the younger woman said something about not having enough time or time being short, something like that, and they left."

"What'd she look like—the younger woman?"

"Oh, dear, the police asked me that and I wasn't much help. It was a while ago. She had dark hair, long, I remember that."

"How old?"

"She was quite a bit younger than Helena. Maybe late twenties, around there." She scrunched her eyes closed in an effort to remember. "I think she was rather small. Not much bigger than you, Carrie."

A sore point. "I'm five three. Not all that small," I muttered.

"Well, she was about that. Pretty. Pretty eyes. She was wearing a hat and a long black coat, and she didn't smile or talk much."

I gave up trying to find a spot on the street and pulled into the lot in back of my building. "I should've dropped you in front of Meg's. I'll walk over with you."

"Don't be silly. It's only a block. Nothing's going to happen to me between here and there."

I was late for my first patient, so I didn't argue. "Promise me you'll wait for me to go to your shop."

"I promise."

I watched her walk up the driveway, started to go into my building, then changed my mind and followed her to

41

the street. I stood watching as she pulled her coat close around her to ward off the morning chill, saw her open the door to the café and go inside. The only people I saw in the vicinity were a young woman pushing a baby carriage, who went into the market, and a man wearing a hat and a well-cut overcoat, who'd been absorbed looking in the window of the estate jewelry store and, as I watched, seemed to make up his mind. As he entered the shop, I thought some lucky woman was on her way to getting a very nice gift.

I didn't have to worry about being late. My first patient didn't show. I'd had five patients scheduled, two of whom had left messages on my machine, canceling. I knew what that was about. A pain clinic had opened in Closter, and they were offering full service: medical consults, massage therapy, physical therapy, acupuncture, and biofeedback, all covered by insurance. Before Rich left I'd worked part-time at a clinic like that, and I understood the advantages. My patients have to pay me out of their pockets. Not being an M.D., I can't bill insurance, plus my pain patients have to go elsewhere for the other therapies. I do better with the Attention Deficit kids, but I'm losing some of them to psychologists and psychiatrists, who can collect from insurance companies for affiliated disorders. I riffled through the pile of bills accumulating on my desk as I waited for my second patient, who was now my first and not due till ten, and thought about my situation. My alimony from Rich would run out in a few years. Sooner or later I was going to have to bite the bullet and either find a psychologist to work with or go to work for a hospital or one of the private pain clinics.

Maybe I could get a job as a P.I., I thought glumly. I seem to have more success at solving crimes than building my biofeedback practice. Not that any brilliant ideas had occurred to me regarding this one. Of course, there was always that other option. I could marry Ted and combine incomes. The option wasn't open-ended, I knew. Besides which, if I decided to marry Ted, money wouldn't be the reason why.

As if reading my mind, the phone rang and Ted's voice interrupted my reveries.

"Hi. Sorry to bother you at work. I thought Franny would pick up."

"She's at Meg's Place. I thought she'd be more comfortable waiting there. I'm meeting her for lunch, and then we're going over to her shop."

"What time?"

"My twelve-fifteen canceled. Assuming my eleven-thirty shows, I can be at the café by twelve-thirty."

"I'll meet you at Franny's shop at one. Wait for me."

"What's going on? Why—"

But the line went dead.

"And you have a nice morning too," I grumbled, dropping the receiver back in its cradle.

I didn't have time to dwell on Ted's abruptness, because the bell rang and I buzzed Ellie Frank in. She's been retired against her will and is having panic attacks, which hit her hardest in the mornings when it's time to get up and go to work and she has no place to go. Panic attacks are one of the things I'm really good at, having survived a few of my own. It's a disorder at which therapists in the pain clinics generally suck big-time, so I don't have to worry about losing her to them.

After Ellie, I saw Arnold Bedrozian. Arnie's seeing me and a psychologist to deal with his depression over the breakup of his marriage, another disorder with which I have mucho experience. So he's signed on for the duration.

Briana Johnson came promptly at eleven-thirty. She's a beautiful young black woman in her early thirties, married to an abusive man who she won't leave, because in the religion she practices a divorced woman is comparable to a fallen woman, besides which she has three children and no money. I suggested professional counseling, but her husband refuses to see anyone but their pastor, whose only advice has been that Briana should try harder not to make her husband angry. I have to bite my tongue to keep from suggesting Briana hire a hit man. Today there was a new wrinkle: a swollen purple eye, carefully masked with makeup. She saw the expression on my face.

"I bumped into a—"

"A fist," I finished for her.

She avoided my eyes, and I let the silence grow between us. "He didn't mean it," she said finally.

I choked back my rage. "Briana," I said, "you can't let this go on. He's going to kill you one day. What'll happen to your children then?"

"It was my fault," she whispered. "I made him mad."

I found myself clenching and unclenching my fists. "Really. How'd you do that?"

"He told me to clean out the closets, but our daughter was sick and I didn't get to it."

Am I fighting a losing battle here? I thought in dismay.

"I still love him," she added, tears pooling in her eyes.

And there was the rub. "Oh, Briana." I shook my head. "He's not capable of loving you or anyone, including your children."

The tears spilled over. "He's their father. Whatever's wrong must be my fault. I've failed him in some way. It's up to me to fix it."

Where had I heard those words? Was it possible something similar had come out of my own mouth not so very long ago?

I once saw a TV show where one of the male characters defined the difference between men and women. "It's our dicks make us stupid," he'd said. "Your hearts do it to you."

Somebody should put that on a bumper sticker.

Three quarters of an hour later, still shaking with anger and frustration, I was on my way to Meg's Place when I noticed a decorative comb studded with pink and red jewels in the window of a boutique. Visions of Allie in a hot-pink kimono, her jet-black hair piled atop her head, the perfect setting for the piece, propelled me inside. Twenty-five hard-earned dollars later, the comb wrapped in tissue paper inside my handbag, I continued on to the café. I was feeling better. Nothing like spending a few bucks to get your mind off your problems. Chocolate works for me too, though I'd never admit that addiction to my patients. I pushed open the door to the café, found Franny at a table in the corner, and plopped myself down beside her.

"I'm starved. You mind if I have a sandwich?" I wiggled out of my jacket and hung it over the back of the chair. "My ADDs don't start coming till two-thirty, so we'll have plenty of time."

"Of course not."

"How about you?" I waved to Meg, who was tending to some customers at the bar.

"I already ate. Try the crab and avocado on pita. It's wonderful."

Betsy materialized at my elbow, and I noticed Franny surreptitiously drop her napkin over the piece of paper on which she'd been writing. I ordered the pita-bread sandwich with a Diet Coke.

"Wait'll you see what I got for Allie." I reached inside my purse and pulled out the comb. "It's not the genuine article, but I think it's smashing."

Franny examined the comb and pronounced it just the thing. "I have a beautiful red obi sash scrolled with pink," she said. "If I can find it, Allie's very welcome to wear it."

"She'd better get that part," I laughed, "or I've blown this week's entire entertainment budget for nothing."

Franny smiled, but I could see she was preoccupied. I gestured toward the paper. "What've you been writing?"

She glanced nervously around the room before removing the napkin, shielding the paper with her hand.

"I've been drawing," she whispered, "trying to sketch the star tattoo." She pushed it in front of me. "I'm not a very good artist, but see those spikes? They look like little castles, don't they?"

They did. It's not the same as the one that came through your mail slot, though," I said. "This has eight points, and it looks more like a snowflake than a star." I folded the paper and handed it back to her. "You should give this to Ted. He's going to meet us at your shop, by the way."

"Why?" She began folding the paper into smaller and smaller sections. "I've told him everything I can remember."

"You're sure you told him about the argument?"

"Of course."

"What that woman said about time, that could be significant."

"I told him everything, so why does he want to talk to me again?"

"I'm sure he just wants to look around the shop or something," I said lamely.

"What would he want to do that for? Does he suspect me?"

"Don't be silly. It's just routine."

I thought back to the time Ted was investigating Erica's murder and was questioning me. *"Just routine,"* he'd said, when I was probably number one on his suspect list.

Meg showed up just then with my sandwich and Coke and pulled up a chair. "Eat, bubbela," she said placing the sandwich in front of me. "You're skin and bones."

I laughed both at Meg's Yiddish and at the allusion to my being undernourished, which I haven't been since I recovered from Rich's abdication. It even earned a smile from Franny and broke the tension. *Bubbela* is not part of Meg's ethnic heritage. She's as Irish as the Riverdancers. Her hair is a shiny red-gold, her eyes a striking turquoise, her skin luminous, and her figure definitely not skin and bones. She's got five or six inches on me, and I've gotten quite used to being totally eclipsed by her beauty when we're together. She's also a marvelous photographer and an excellent cook. It's grossly unfair, and if it wasn't that she's about the best person I know, I'd refuse to have anything to do with her.

"Yes, Mother," I replied and dutifully polished off the sandwich. When I'd swallowed the last delectable bite, I looked up and saw that Meg had unfolded Franny's sketch and was studying it. Betsy came over to clear the table, and Franny grabbed the paper and pushed it into her tote bag.

"Ted's meeting us at the shop at one," I said, glancing at my watch. "We'd better get going. You want to come?"

"Can't," she replied. "I don't like leaving Betsy alone with the lunch crowd."

"Okay. C'mon, Franny." I dropped six dollars onto the table and put on my jacket. "See you later."

Meg was on her way to the kitchen as Franny and I left. Betsy waved. I waved back.

"It didn't take Meg long to replace me," Franny said unhappily as we walked down the street.

"She didn't replace you. She'll be thrilled to have you back whenever you're ready. Betsy's just an extra pair of hands so she can spend more time with Kevin."

Franny looked hopeful. "Did she tell you that?"

"Of course." She hadn't used exactly those words, but I felt certain Meg would soon be able to employ two part-timers. Meg's Place was becoming almost as popular as Xaviars and Freelance Café down the street, which are where I would like to believe all good gourmands get to eat when they die and go to heaven.

Ted's unmarked brown Chevy was parked outside Golden Oldies when we arrived. He got out when he saw us. He was carrying a folder, and his greeting to us was short and sweet. Well, short.

"Hi. Let's go in. I want Franny to look at some more pictures."

I gave Franny a nudge. "See, I told you. Routine stuff."

She dug out her key, opened the door, and we trooped inside. The little shop smelled musty and dank, as if it had been weeks, not days, that it had been closed. Unopened mail was scattered like confetti on the floor in front of the mail slot. Clearly Franny hadn't been near the place since the night she'd found the star. She gathered up the mail and dropped it into a wicker basket.

"You want me to go through that for you?" I asked her. "There might be something important."

"Like another warning?"

I grinned at Ted. "Well, if there is we've got Dirty Harry here to protect us."

"Leave it for now," Dirty Harry said. "I'll go through it before I go." He was at Franny's desk and had opened his folder. "Franny, I want you to look carefully at these photographs. Tell me if any of the women look like the woman who came in with Helena Forester that day."

Franny reached into her tote bag for her glasses, perched them on her nose, and sat down at the desk. Ted stood looking over her shoulder, and I found a straight-back Shaker rocking chair and took a load off my feet. Franny carefully studied the pictures. One after the other she turned them over, shaking her head.

"I'm sorry," she said to Ted. It's not any of them."

"Who are they?" I asked Ted.

"Distant relatives, coworkers from the foundation and her travel agency, anyone whose picture we could dig up who had any connection with her." He pulled one last photograph from the folder. "This one's a long shot," he said to Franny. "She look at all familiar?"

I got up, picked my way around a hodgepodge of stuff to the desk, and gazed down at the photograph. It was a little fuzzy, as though it had been enlarged, a full-face black-and-white shot of a pretty young woman of about seventeen or eighteen. She had long dark brown hair framing an oval face with high cheekbones and a squarish chin. The eyes were almond-shaped, brown, with long lashes, the nose small, and the lips full and curved in a smile.

"It's an old photo," Ted said, "taken from a high-school yearbook."

Franny walked over to the glass-paneled door and held the photograph up to the light. "I'm not sure," she said after a minute.

"Take your time," Ted responded. "Think older. Ten years or more."

She pushed her wire-rimmed glasses closer to her face. "I think it's the woman who was with Helena. This girl is much younger, her face is fuller, but the eyes—the eyes look the same." She looked up at Ted. "Who is she?"

"Name's Laurel Herman."

I caught my breath. Ted's eyes flashed to me, then back to Franny. "She's Helena Forester's stepdaughter," he said.

"Well," Franny said, continuing to study the photo. "That would make sense, then, that she'd have been with her."

"Not in this case," Ted replied.

Franny looked up. "What do you mean?"

Ted was looking at me when he answered. "Helena Forester and she haven't spoken since a year or two after Laurel's father died. How'd you know the name, Carrie?"

Damn him. Nothing ever gets by him. I tried to keep my face impassive. "I didn't—I—think I read something about her in the paper. What happened between her and Forester?"

He didn't believe me for a minute. "It seems Ms. Herman's father's will left his entire estate to Ms. Forester."

The bastard! This Jenny hadn't told me.

"Oh, my, how terrible," Franny gasped. "How could a father cut off his child?"

The words were out before I thought. "He's a man. His dick made him stupid."

Franny blushed and looked away. Ted shot me one of his "I must be insane to put up with this" looks.

"Present company excepted, of course," I added ingratiatingly.

He started gathering up the photos. "You and I need to talk, *mon petit chou.*"

In case your French is rusty, that's a term of endearment meaning *dear* or *darling*, but directly translated it means *my little cabbage* or *little cabbage head*. I have an idea Ted was using the term literally, but I let it go, figuring I'd pushed his buttons enough for one day. I moved to what I thought was safer ground. "Was there an autopsy done on Laurel's mother?"

"What are you driving at?"

"Just that it seems strange—Laurel's father marrying Helena so soon after her mother died and then leaving nothing to his daughter—"

"Did I say anything about Laurel's mother?"

Oh, shit. "I—no—didn't you—I must've read that in the paper."

"Uh-huh. You must let me know what newspaper you subscribe to. I'd be interested in talking to their sources." He turned away from me and spoke directly to Franny. "I'll take a quick look through your mail now, just to make sure there's nothing."

Franny brought him the basket and he spent several minutes flipping through the pile. When he'd finished, he smiled at Franny. "Just like mine. Nothing but junk and bills." He rose. "Gotta get back."

"Oh, wait," Franny said. "I almost forgot." She reached into her tote bag and handed him the crumpled sketch. "That's as close as I could get to the star tattoo. I thought it might be helpful."

"Yeah," he said, smoothing the paper out, "this is good. Thanks." He pocketed it and walked to the door. "What time do you finish today, Carrie?"

"About six, but I have to pick up Franny and bring her—"

"I'll be at your house at six-thirty."

Control freak. All sugar and honey, I inquired, "Is that a dinner invitation?"

"Depends," he shot back, raking me with his eyes, "on whether you call eating crow dinner."

He was gone before I could think of a suitable reply.

I expected Franny to ask what all that had been about, but the exchange had apparently gone right past her. We spent the next hour on a treasure hunt, moving things around, pawing through endless piles, much of which looked to me like junk my grandmother would have thrown out.

"How do you ever find anything in here?" I asked in frustration.

Franny's eyes sparkled, making her look ten years younger. "That's the fun of it," she said. "Sometimes I forget what I have, and when I come across it again it's like a new discovery."

Which just goes to prove that old saying about one man's meat being another man's poison. I'm not known for my neatness and organizational skills, but all this clutter would drive me nuts. In the end, though, we came up with three gloriously colorful Japanese fans, a delicate green and pink flowered parasol, the red silk brocade obi, which was breathtakingly gorgeous—and a wicked-looking curved sword, the ideal prop for Ko-Ko, the Lord High Executioner. I unsheathed it and ran my finger delicately over the edge. "Ah, just the thing if the local critic gives them a bad review."

Bad joke. Franny didn't smile. I tried to extricate my foot. "Uh, listen, I'll put these things in my trunk and pick you up at Meg's after work. Okay?"

She didn't answer. Me and my big mouth, reminding her of the murder just when I'd gotten her interested in something else. "Come on, I'll walk you to Meg's."

"I think I'll stay here for a while, Carrie."

Uh-oh. "Maybe you'd rather come with me to the office. Ruth-Ann'll be there by now and—"

She was irritated. "I'm not a child. I don't need a baby-sitter."

How to tell her I was following orders? Already on Ted's shit list, I didn't feel like adding to my mea culpas. But I didn't want to add to her fears either.

"I'll tell you what. You come to the office with me now, and I'll call the community theater and see if I can set up an appointment with the director. If he's free I'll have Ruth-Ann run you over. If you're going to do props for the show, you'll need a list of what to look for."

She hesitated, then reluctantly acquiesced. I knew what was bothering her. Franny had always prided herself on managing on her own. I understood that. It was degrading to her self-esteem to find herself having to lean on others. I did my best to reassure her.

"There're times we all need help from our friends, you know, Franny. I don't know what I'd've done without

Meg during my divorce and that terrible time when I was suspected of killing Erica. I'm just glad I was able to be there for her last year. It's no disgrace to lean on other people when you're going through rough times."

"I know. But you're busy. You don't need an old woman disturbing your household. You work and you have two children and a boyfriend. . . ."

At the moment the boyfriend was debatable, but that was my problem. "You're not disturbing anything. Allie loves sleeping with me." I didn't mention that sleeping with Allie was like sleeping with an octopus. Sleeping with Ted, on the other hand, had considerably more to offer. So why did I keep messing up? I shook my head and brought my attention back to Franny. "Come on. If I have a cancelation I'll hook you up and we'll do a stress-management exercise. You'll feel like a new woman."

Gathering the props we'd collected in one arm, holding the sword at arm's length in the other, I opened the door and started down the steps. And almost dropped the lot. Because on the sidewalk outside Franny's shop, a two-foot chalk outline of a four-pointed star—a nearly exact replica of the one in the shoe box—stared me in the face. In the center was a crudely drawn figure of a monkey, this time with its paws over its eyes. I couldn't suppress a gasp. The star had become as obscene to me as a swastika. Behind me I heard Franny whimper. Backing up the steps, I pushed her into the shop and slammed the door. I stood with my back against it, breathing hard, as I let the props slide to the floor from hands gone limp with shock.

I looked at Franny, who had her hand pressed against her heart and had turned a sickly greenish-white. I forced myself to move. "Sit down, Franny," I commanded. As she sank down onto the rocker, I saw her eyes roll up into her head. I pushed her head down between her legs. "Breathe. Take deep breaths from your diaphragm. You are not going to faint!"

I was down on my knees rubbing her hands to bring back circulation when the color began creeping back into her face and she raised her head.

"I'm all right," she murmured. "It was just such a shock seeing that thing there."

I was about to spout my litany about its not being a life-threatening situation but caught myself. Because it was. "You're not going to let this psycho make you sick," I muttered instead.

My mind was racing, outpacing my heart, which was thumping like the little drummer boy against the walls of my chest. Crossing back to the door, I drew the curtain over the glass panel and threw the bolt. I parted the curtain a crack and peered out. Was the person who'd made that repulsive drawing still around? Probably. He had to have been watching the shop, waiting for Ted to leave. And he had to have watched for an opportune moment when no one was on the street. Why was he doing this? He was taking a chance on being seen. If it had been to scare Franny, he'd already done that. The significance of the monkey with its paws over its eyes. See no evil. Franny had seen the evil, but she apparently hadn't seen enough to endanger the perpetrator. That was the irony. He didn't know that. The person was taking more of a chance on being identified than if he had just disappeared. Maybe someone in a neighboring store had seen him, would be able to describe him. It takes time to chalk a picture on the sidewalk. I'd have to ask around. But not now. I'd put that on tomorrow's agenda. Today's dilemma was to get out of here in one piece. I prodded my sluggish brain into devising a plan. "You have a back door, don't you, Franny?"

Her voice had lost resonance, gone wispy with fright. "Up the back stairs through my apartment," she got out.

"You okay now? Can you walk?"

She nodded and got shakily to her feet. I handed her the parasol and the fans. "You carry these." I wound the obi around my waist to free my hands and unsheathed the sword. Don't ask me what I intended to do with it if someone jumped us, but lacking Ruth-Ann's pepper spray, it was the best I could come up with for protection. "Show me the way."

Like a couple of cat burglars, we crept up the dusty stairs to the apartment above. Every creaky step caused my heart to flutter, every figure or sculpture in the dark apartment cast ominous, threatening shadows. I followed Franny through the living room, through her tiny kitchen to the back hallway, down the back stairs, and out to the loading area in the rear of her shop. And then we sprinted, Franny clutching the fans and waving the parasol in front of her like a bayonet, me, obi trailing, brandishing the sword. Fortunately we were in the back of the buildings so no one saw us, or they might have called the cops, who would certainly have shipped us off to Bellevue. I glanced anxiously at Franny, afraid she'd have a heart attack from sheer terror and exertion, but to tell the awful truth, we covered the three-building distance between my office and her shop running neck and neck. What had happened to my New Year's resolution to join Meg in her tae kwon do class? I was panting like Horty after a game of Frisbee as I jerked open the door to my building.

"We'll take the elevator," I gasped, pressing the button. The door opened, and a woman wearing some endangered species and a diamond the size of a golf ball stepped out. A look of consternation passed over her face as she took in our appearance.

I don't know what came over me. I'd like to think it was a touch of insanity brought on by trauma and the outrageous size of that woman's ring. I picked up the corner of the red obi and began wiping the blade of the sword as if cleaning off blood. "Okay," I stage-whispered to Franny, "if it's so important to you, you can have a finger. But I have dibs on the thumb." Giving the blade a final inspection, I blew on it and flipped it into its sheath.

Franny was so stunned she just stared at me openmouthed. The woman took off like she was being pursued by hounds from hell. I fell onto the floor of the elevator and whooped with laughter. "Sorry, Franny, sorry," I gasped between giggles. "Terror brings out the screwball in me." Too bad Meg wasn't here. Franny thought I was crazy. Meg would've joined in the lunacy.

No patients were in the waiting room when the elevator door opened. The room was a shambles, books and toys all over the floor. Jimmy Lee had obviously been dropped off by his mother. By the time Ruth-Ann came out of my office, I'd gotten myself under control. I'd taken off the obi, stored the props in the closet, and settled Franny in an armchair in the corner.

Attired in her usual midcalf-length skirt and high-neck blouse, her ebony hair pulled back in a bun, Ruth-Ann looked lovelier than ever. She'd achieved her goal of one hundred and fifteen pounds, down from one sixty-five last year, and was growing into a beautiful young woman. She wore no makeup except a pale lip-stick. I wasn't sure if that was a religious directive or a personal choice, but with her vivid coloring she didn't need it anyway.

"You're late," she said reprovingly. "You have a mes-sage to call a new patient, a Mr. Yoshida, and I have Jimmy hooked up. You know what he can do to this room when his mother doesn't wait with him."

"Even when she does," I mumbled, running a quick comb through my hair. "I'll help you pick up later. Would you make Franny a cup of tea while I work with Jimmy? She's a little upset. Oh, by the way, tell her where you get your pepper spray."

Ruth-Ann's mouth opened in surprise as I disappeared into my office.

I'd just finished with my last patient and was cleaning off the sensors when the phone rang. It was Jenny, tell-ing me she'd gotten the job at Saatchi and Saatchi, was feeling great, and would be moving back to the city, so she wouldn't be seeing me anymore. I was glad for her but felt a pang at having lost another patient. I wished her luck and told her to keep in touch, let me know how she was doing. "Oh, by the way, Jenny," I added casu-ally. "You never did tell me why you hated Helena For-ester."

"Well, it's no secret that my parents' friendship with Laurel's father ended when he married Helena," she re-plied after a moment's hesitation, "so I was never one of her most favorite people. But one night last year a date took me to a charity dinner. It was a formal affair for, I think, Unicef or Save the World's Children, something like that. She was there dressed to the nines, and everyone was making a big fuss of her. Andrew, her husband, was at our table, so he asked me to dance a couple of times while she was off getting stroked. He's a very attractive man, fun to talk to, but that's all there was to it. I don't get involved with married men, and I'd have to be brain dead to start up with anyone connected to Helena. When we were leaving, he thanked us for coming and helped me on with my coat. Maybe held on to my hand a little longer than necessary. I wasn't even aware she'd noticed. I never saw him after that night, but suddenly I got let go in a supposed company bloodbath, and all the doors at the other agencies were closed to me."

"But you can't really believe she had anything to do with—"

"I sure can. That jerk, Andrew, called me and apologized. I was furious. He knew what she was like. He should have kept his mitts off me."

"You mean to tell me she would've been able to influence—"

"She used her money like a cudgel to get whatever she wanted. You'd be surprised at all the people who didn't want to cross her."

I lowered my voice to make sure Franny couldn't hear from the other room. "Do you still see your friend—her first husband's daughter?"

Her voice became suspicious. "Why?"

"I'd like to meet her. Could you arrange it?"

"What for? I don't see—"

"She could be in trouble, Jenny, unless she has an airtight alibi for that Wednesday."

"Don't be ridiculous. She hasn't been in touch with Helena for years."

"Yes, she has. She was with her just a few weeks ago at an antique shop here in Piermont."

There was a heavy silence on the other end of the line, which I finally broke. "I'd like to help her if I can."

"Seems to me you'd be more likely to want to help your boyfriend."

"I just want to talk to her. If she had nothing to do with Helena Forester's death, I could be a strong ally."

A long pause. I was waiting for her to say who did I think I was kidding, but lady luck smiled.

"Why should you want to get involved?"

Why did I? Partially, I guess, because vis-à-vis Franny I already was involved and I wanted the perpetrator caught, but partly, I had to admit, I was hooked. I wanted to see how all these disparate puzzle pieces fit together. I struggled to find an answer that would be convincing, decided on the truth, except for the hooked part.

"Whoever did this is stalking a friend of mine. She's an elderly woman, the nicest person you'd ever want to meet. She's very frightened. I want to talk to Laurel because she might know something that could help find the killer. The police know she was with Helena that day in the antique shop. They'll catch up with her eventually. It can't hurt her to talk to me before that happens, and it might help."

There was a long pause. Then, "I'll see what I can do. I'll get back to you tomorrow."

"Tomorrow's Wednesday. I won't be in the office. Can you—"

"I'll leave a message on your machine." She hung up.

* * *

Franny and I were putting on our coats when the bell rang. We both jumped. Standing in the hallway when I opened the door was a middle-age Japanese man of average height, wearing a business suit and carrying his coat and a briefcase.

"Dr. Carlin?" he inquired in perfect English.

Lots of people make that mistake and I usually go into a detailed explanation about my not being a doctor, but this guy was a stranger and I was still jittery from this afternoon's experience. "I'm Carrie Carlin," I said shortly. "Can I help you?"

He smiled politely. "I'm sorry to disturb you. I called earlier and spoke with your secretary. My name is Yoshida. I'd like to make an appointment to see you tomorrow. Would that be convenient?"

Bad timing, but a patient is a patient. "I'm not in the office on Wednesdays, but I'd be happy to see you on Thursday. Please come in. We'll just be a minute, Franny," I called over my shoulder as Mr. Yoshida followed me into my office. I crossed to my desk and ran my finger down my appointment schedule for Thursday, found several slots open. "How's ten o'clock?"

"That would be fine."

"Can I ask who referred you to me?"

"The people at the pain center in Nyack. I have whiplash from an automobile accident. It's been causing me a good deal of discomfort. They told me you work wonders with pain patients."

Praise indeed when it comes from old colleagues. Either that or Mr. Yoshida was one of the difficult ones on whom they'd given up.

"Have you ever done biofeedback?" I asked.

"No, but I meditate."

"Good, then we're halfway there."

I gave him a friendly professional smile and we walked back into the reception area. Franny was stacking the *Mikado* props on one of the chairs. The red and pink silk obi was draped over the back.

Mr. Yoshida stopped in front of it. "What a magnificent obi," he commented admiringly.

"It's for an operetta that my daughter's auditioning for," I said. "This is Mrs. Gold. She runs the antique shop down the street. She's thinking of helping with props."

He bowed politely to Franny, reached out, and ran his fingers gently over the brocade, then noticed the sword Franny was taking out of the closet. "May I see that?"

Rather reluctantly, Franny handed it to him. "It's quite old," she murmured. "It was part of an estate."

Turning it over, he studied the carving on the handle, then placed it carefully on the chair seat. "It's a beauty. Is it for sale?"

"Perhaps after the production is over."

"When will that be?"

Anxious to get going, I began rolling the obi and gathering up the rest of the props. "In about three or four weeks, I believe. I don't have the exact dates."

"Well, you must let me know. Maybe you and I can do business," he said to Franny.

As we rode down in the elevator, Franny smiled and said, "I'll be open on the weekend. If you're in the neighborhood, please stop by. I might have other things you'd be interested in."

He nodded pleasantly and we parted at the top of the driveway.

"Maybe you should sell the sword to him now, Franny," I said as we hurried around to the back of the building. "A sale's a sale, and who knows if he'll still want it in a month?"

"No, if Allie gets the part, I want them to have it for the show."

I unlocked the trunk and carefully placed the props inside. It was getting dark, and we were both anxious to get into the safety of the car, although neither of us voiced our fear.

"The director may not even want to use it unless he can figure out a way to mask the blade," I said as I started the engine and drove onto the street.

"It shouldn't be hard. I imagine any kind of thick tape ought to do it."

We were chattering to keep from staring at the sidewalk in front of Franny's store as we drove past. I kept my eyes on the road, but in the end I couldn't help it. "Is it still there?" I whispered.

"Yes," she replied.

5

✦

TED WAS IN THE LIVING ROOM playing a game of chess with Matt when we arrived home. I was dying to tell him about the chalked star, but I was anxious to hear how Allie's audition had gone and figured the longer I could avoid the impending discussion about the source of my information, the better. So after dropping a quick kiss on both heads, I headed for the stairs. "Be right down, you two. Franny and I want to talk to Allie." Allie came charging down the stairs before we'd gone halfway up. I knew by her face the news was good and breathed a sigh of relief.

"I'm Pitti-Sing." She beamed.

"Oh, honey, that's wonderful." I gave her a hug. "I'm not in the least surprised. The director would've had to be blind and deaf not to cast you. Let me just put on my slippers and you'll tell us all about it while I make dinner."

Franny joined in. "I'm so thrilled for you, Allie," she said warmly. "Congratulations."

"What's going on? Are congratulations in order?" Ted called from downstairs.

"You bet," I yelled back. "We have here a budding star. You can stay for dinner so long as you don't spoil our celebration with shoptalk."

That should keep him off my back for the time being, I thought with satisfaction. Ted was always careful around the children. He wouldn't give me hell in front of them.

At my urging, Franny went up to Allie's room to lie down before dinner. She was still pretty shaken, although she was dealing with it much better than she had been. Being surrounded by friends was helping her cope. My own nervousness was becoming edged with an odd sense of excitement. *Am I a danger addict?* I shook off the thought. Despite the crazy situations in which I've found myself, I've never been a high-risk kind of person. Point in fact, I wasn't taking the leap into matrimony. Or, other than sending my yearly contribution, saving any beached whales either.

I made shepherd's pie for dinner. It had a double advantage: I was able to stretch a pound and a half of ground beef to feed five people, plus it gave Allie and me a chance to talk.

"I was so nervous, Mom. I swear my tongue got stuck to the roof of my mouth."

"Well, you obviously got it unstuck." I wiped my eyes as I sliced the onions and dumped them into the pan. "God, I hate chopping onions."

She laughed, putting all that teenage enthusiasm and energy into whipping the potatoes. "I sang better than anyone except Sophie Maitini. She got Yum-Yum."

"Do I know her?"

"No, she doesn't go to Northern Valley. She's older, only moved here a little while ago. She's got the most beautiful voice—like Sarah Brightman."

"Really. That's quite a compliment coming from you."

"She doesn't act like her, though. She's not friendly. Doesn't talk to anybody."

"Well, if she's new—"

"It's not that, I don't think. I guess she's just snooty."

"Well," I admonished her, as I added salt and pepper to the mixture, "don't make snap judgments. Maybe she's shy. Is she pretty?"

"Yeah. Small, though. I tower over her."

"You tower over me too."

She laughed. "Everybody towers over you, Mom, but even you are taller than Sophie."

I made a face. "Pitti-Sing's the next best female role, isn't it?"

"Except Katisha. But I'm too young. And she's a contralto. Of course, Pitti-Sing's a mezzo, but I can handle that."

I started layering the beef-and-onion mixture with the potatoes and peas. "Well, I have a terrific surprise for you. I didn't want to tell you about it till I was sure you got the part."

"What? Tell me what?"

"When I told Franny about the show, she got all enthusiastic and said she'd like to do props. You know she has all this great stuff in her shop, so I told her I'd ask you about talking to the director, and this afternoon we came up with some fantastic Japanese things. And I bought you something you're going to love. I'll show you everything after dinner."

"Oh, Mom, that's not fair. I can't wait till then. The pie still has to cook. Show me now."

"Sweetie, the props're still in the car. If I don't get this pie in the oven, we'll be eating at midnight."

"I'll get them." She was jumping up and down, eyes sparkling, so happy and excited that I gave in.

"Okay, take my car key out of my bag on the hall table. The stuff's in the trunk. I left the garage door open. Close it after you and come in the front door. And put on your jacket." Our garage isn't attached to the house, and normally the kids complain if they have to go out in the cold to retrieve any packages I've failed to bring in, but Allie was motivated. She was gone in a flash and I started humming, "Oh, willow, titwillow, titwillow," as I dotted the last layer of potato with butter and put it in the oven. Drying my hands on a towel, I wandered into the living room to see how the game was progressing. I looked at the two bent heads and felt my heart twist. Ted was so good with Matt, better than Rich, who never seemed to have time for chess or any other game lately. Why did I keep finding excuses not to make this arrangement permanent?

"Who's winning?" I asked.

Nobody moved.

"Shh, Mom, I'm thinking," Matt grunted. "Don't break my concentration."

"I beg your pardon. Don't mind me. I'm just the cook." I sat down next to Ted and put my hand on his leg, hoping to break his concentration. I'm pretty sure I did, but before he could react, the front door opened and Allie blew in, arms full, kicking the door shut behind her. "Somebody help me." I jumped up and took the sword and parasol from her. She followed me into the living room, where we dropped the loot onto the couch beside Ted. When she was hanging her jacket in the closet she called out, "You're the best mom." She came over to me and kissed me on the cheek, not a common occurrence lately. "That was really cute what was on the trunk."

"You mean what was in the trunk," I said as I unrolled the obi.

"No, I mean the star you drew for me on your trunk. Of course, I'm not the star of the show, you know. And you're not really a very good artist. Don't you know stars have five points?"

The obi slipped from my grasp.

By the time I remembered the shepherd's pie, it had burned to a crisp. Ted called in his cohorts from the crime unit and they took photographs and dusted my car for prints, even though Ted didn't expect they'd find any but mine and Allie's. Then he and they took off for Franny's shop. I ordered pizza for the kids and tried to make light of the situation. Franny sat quietly, not eating and not saying anything, but I knew she was a wreck. I was pretty shook up myself. It was clear Franny wasn't the only target anymore. The perp had made the connection between Franny and me, and he knew she was staying here. It put all of us in danger, and I had to face the fact that this included my children. I wasn't happy about it. Ted wasn't either, and when he came back to the house, he decided we needed police protection and stayed over.

After I got the kids to bed, we talked far into the night. I'd waited for Allie to fall asleep, then tiptoed downstairs and made up the couch for Ted and me. Ironic how situations reverse. Imagine having to sneak around to sleep with your lover when you're an adult. But I'm stuck with the values pounded into my head by an old-fashioned father who raised me alone, and Ted and me in bed together is just not something I'm ready for my children to see.

"I never should've had you bring Franny here," he said. "It's too dangerous. We're going to have to find somewhere else for her to stay."

"What're you planning to do—give her a new identity and put her in the witness-protection program?"

"This is no joke, Carrie." He rolled on his side and took my hand. "What would you think about sending the kids to stay with Rich till we catch this creep?"

"Oh, my God, that's the last thing I'd want to do. He'll go ballistic."

"But if he knows they could be in danger—"

"Do you really think they are?"

He was quiet for a minute. "No, not if we take reasonable precautions. This guy's got nothing to gain by threatening your children. You really worried about Rich's reaction?"

"He'll use it against me—against us, if we ever—"

"Yeah? What?"

"You know . . . if we ever get—or live together—or anything," I mumbled into my pillow.

He released my hand. "Christ, you can't even get the word out, can you?"

"I—that's not—can we stick to the subject?"

"Fine. Rich is living with whatsername, the infant with the Marilyn Monroe voice."

"Suzanne. According to the court he can do whatever he wants. I can't. I'm getting alimony."

"Are you telling me he objects to your seeing me?"

I sighed. "It's an excuse, Ted. He doesn't want me, but it bothers him that I'm seeing someone—that I'm not still pining over him and have moved on. So he makes a big deal over the fact you're a cop."

"Your kids aren't in danger because I'm a cop, Carrie."

"I know that." I could feel my face flushing. "It's me. I swear I'm a magnet. I don't know what—"

"You're not so much a magnet as you are a buttinsky." Without seeing his face I knew he'd relented and was smiling. I also knew what was coming. "This might be a good time to tell me just what it is you know about Laurel Herman and how you got your information."

I hesitated. "Honestly, I'm not trying to be difficult. It's—I'm kind of bound by professional ethics. Something was told to me by one of my patients and—"

Impatience crept into his voice. "You're not a lawyer or a doctor. I don't think privileged information applies to you."

"You're wrong," I responded hotly, propping myself up on my elbow. "I'm a professional. People tell me—"

"I'm wrong? Are you aware that even the Secret Service can be hauled into court and forced to testify?"

He had me there. "I read the papers. But people tell me things in confidence. They have a right to expect—"

"What? That you'll help obstruct a murder investigation?"

"Yes! No—I mean—look, the patient is going to call me tomorrow. Let me talk to her. I really can't see why she'd object—"

"She. Well, that's a start anyway."

I clamped my mouth shut before Jenny's name slipped out. Ted laughed softly. He reached up and pulled me back down, wrapping his arms around me. I snuggled up against him, feeling safe, needing to feel safe. Hating myself for the need.

"I'll hold off dragging you to the precinct for one more day," he whispered into my hair, "but after that, you'd better come clean or else."

"Or else you'll subpoena me to testify before the grand jury, right?" I murmured against his chest, comforted by the protuberance I could feel under his pillow that was his gun, turned on by the one prodding me that wasn't. I reached for him. "I'll invoke executive privilege."

He woke me with kisses, a vast improvement over Lucie's or Horty's or the alarm clock's wail. He was showered and dressed. I hadn't heard a thing. I'd slept deeply, dreamlessly, like somebody'd slipped a mickey into my drink. Which goes to show what having a sex life'll do for you.

"It's six-thirty," he whispered. "I'm taking off."

I caught his arm. "Wait. I forgot to ask you last night. Have you talked to the husband—the present one? If ever anybody had a motive—"

"He was teaching a class. About twenty-five kids can attest to it."

"He could've hired someone."

"Certainly not out of the question. He's not off the hook by a long shot, though I did see him shed a few tears at the funeral."

"So he's an accomplished actor. For a couple of million I could fake a good cry."

He leaned over and nuzzled my neck. "So long as that's all you fake."

"I wouldn't let you off that easy." I pulled him down and kissed him. "What'd you think of him?"

"Good-looking guy, pleasant, seemed to want to co-operate. Maybe a little too much."

"What do you mean?"

"Couldn't wait to provide us with an enemy list."

"Ah, so. Who's on it?"

He laughed as he got up and slid his gun into his shoulder holster. "When you graduate from the police academy, I'll be happy to tell you."

"Come on, Ted. Who's on it?"

He shook his head, grinning.

"Well, who else benefits? You can tell me that."

"The will's being read today."

I sat up. "Really? Will you be there?"

"Not sure. One way or another, though, I'll see it."

"And you'll tell me what it says."

"Maybe. When you tell me what *she* said."

I flopped back down. "Get out of here, you black-mailer."

"I'm not blackmailing you. I'm giving you a chance to come forward and do your duty like a good citizen."

"Yeah, yeah."

He bent down and kissed me. "Horty's been out, and I fed the cats. You could catch another half hour. Call you later."

I lay back and closed my eyes. At the door he said, "You still take Wednesdays off, don't you?"

"Yeah. Why?"

"I'm sending someone over this afternoon to install an alarm system. My treat."

My eyes flew open and I sat bolt upright. "Oh, no. I can't allow that."

"It's Slomin's Shield. Don't you listen to the radio commercials? No charge to install. We'll discuss the monthly fee when the bill comes in."

"Ted, I can't afford the monthly charge no matter how little it is. Besides, we have Horty. He's—"

"Horty would lick an intruder to death and you know it."

"I can't let you pay for it," I insisted.

I saw the color creep up over his shirt, knew I was in for it. "Goddammit, why is it so hard for you to let me do something for you? We agreed the kids can stay here, but you've gotta face the fact this guy is unpredictable. What he's doing—stalking you and Franny—that's not the behavior of a person who's got it all together, even a criminal. If you can't accept it for yourself, you have a responsibility to think of Franny and of your kids. Otherwise, you'd damned well better send them to Rich."

That stopped my mouth. I caved in.

As he opened the door, he said in a calmer but chilly voice, "By the way, you might be interested in knowing we've located Laurel Herman. We'll be picking her up later today for questioning."

When I got into my car to drive Allie and Matt to school, no trace of the star remained. An unseen hand, undoubtedly Ted's, had wiped my trunk clean. The kids were uncharacteristically silent; nobody brought up the previous night's events. Wednesday being my errand day, I'd told them I was taking them to school because I had to finish the marketing by noon so I could get home to wait for a delivery. That was true—I needed to be there when the alarm people came. But it was also because I didn't want them waiting out on the street for the car pool. I didn't explain why I'd brought Franny and Horty along, hoping they'd assume I was taking Horty to the vet for his shots. Despite what Ted had said about Horty's propensity for smothering strangers with slurpy kisses, his size does serve as a deterrent. Looking at him, you wouldn't guess he's more of a pussycat than our pussycats. José, the smallest of the trio—and who's about half the size of Horty's leg—is far more formidable. You mess with José at your peril.

"When do rehearsals begin, Allie?" I asked, breaking the silence.

"Next Monday. Three afternoons a week to start."

"Where?"

"At the high school. The community theater's going to use the auditorium."

"That'll work out. I'll pick you up after school today. See if you can arrange for the director to meet with Franny." That took care of Child Number One. Now for Child Number Two. "Mattie, what's your schedule?"

"I got soccer practice."

"Who's driving car pool?"

"Mrs. Moscone, I think."

Tina Moscone had covered me on more than one occasion in the past. Reliable as an old shoe, she never asks unwelcome questions. I'd call her and ask her to get to the field a little early and make sure Matt came home with her.

Feeling relieved that I'd covered all bases, I dropped the kids off at the elementary school.

"You up to a little adventure?" I asked Franny as we pulled away.

I saw panic in her eyes. "I—I'm not sure. You're not thinking of doing anything crazy like your antics with the sword yesterday, are you?"

I laughed. "God, Franny, I didn't mean to freak you out. No, it's nothing like that. What I have in mind is talking to Laurel Herman if I can find out her address from—well, from someone who knows her. You want to come with me, or should I drop you at Meg's?"

"I—I'm not sure."

I started the engine. "Well, make a decision by the time we get to the office. I want to check my messages."

I found a parking spot on the street, directly, as fate would have it, in front of Franny's shop. Our eyes flew to the sidewalk before we'd even opened the car doors. The star was gone—erased, I was sure, by Ted after the photographer had finished his work.

"Well, that's okay, then," I breathed in relief, hanging on to Horty's leash with both hands as he yanked me out of the car. "Why don't you have a cup of coffee at Meg's while I run upstairs? I'll meet you there, and you can let me know what you've decided."

Franny nodded and set off. Only when I saw her open the door to the café did I start for my office, my protector lumbering along beside me.

There were three messages on my machine. The first was Briana's soft voice canceling Friday's appointment. Her husband was taking her away for a long weekend. She would call me to reschedule. I hoped that she was telling me the truth and it wasn't that she had been beaten up and was ashamed to let me see her. I resolved to call her later. The second message was from my boss at the old center, telling me they'd sent me a patient, which I already knew, and the third was a terse message from Jenny.

"Carrie, Laurel and I will meet you this morning at Meg's Place. Nine-thirty. Leave the boyfriend home."

I glanced at my watch. Eight-forty. Plenty of time. I erased the tape, checked my e-mail, and went through my bills. By nine-fifteen I'd finished making my calls. Tina Moscone promised to keep an eye on Matt, and Briana didn't answer. I locked up and took the stairs the three flights down to the street, racing so as not to be dragged by Horty.

I tied his leash to a tree outside the café, told him to guard the tree, and went inside. Franny was sitting at the counter having breakfast with Meg's husband, Kevin. I walked over and planted a kiss on his cheek. "Hi, speed demon. What's new?"

"Nothing nearly as exciting as what I hear is going on in your never uneventful life." He got to his feet and gave me a bear hug. "Franny's been giving me the lowdown."

I hopped up on a bar stool. "Well, hold your hat, it's about to bump up a notch." I turned to Franny. "Guess who's coming to breakfast?"

Franny's dismayed expression made it clear she wasn't as thrilled as I was. "Oh, no. Don't tell me."

"Yup. Message on my machine said my patient is bringing her."

"What are you two talking about? Who's coming?" Meg came out of the kitchen and leaned across the counter, her hand resting affectionately on Kev's arm.

"The long-lost daughter," I said.

The words were barely out of my mouth when the

door opened and Jenny walked in accompanied by a slim woman about my height wearing a long black coat. They hesitated in the doorway as Jenny glanced around searching for me.

"That's her," Franny whispered, clearly distressed. "That's the girl who was with Helena Forester. Oh, my goodness, Carrie, I'm so nervous. Would you mind if I didn't join you?"

"It's okay. Relax. No reason you have to." I slid off the stool and made my way to the door.

"Hi, Jenny," I said. "Thanks for coming." To Laurel I said, "I'm Carrie Carlin. Glad you could make it. Let's grab that table in the corner." I led them to one where we could speak without fear of eavesdroppers and sat with my back against the wall facing the trio at the counter, who were making a great show of pretending not to notice us. Franny resolutely kept her face turned away, but I could see her in the mirror. Jenny and Laurel sat down opposite me. Jenny carelessly tossed her fur-lined leather jacket over the back of her chair. Laurel kept her coat on. I studied her face. She was quite lovely. I remembered that Jenny had told me the mother had been Eurasian and beautiful, and I could see Laurel's heritage in the tilt of her dark eyes and the dusky gold tone of her skin. Her hair was thick and long, dark brown with chestnut highlights.

I saw Meg signal Betsy, who seconds later appeared, menus in hand, at my side. "I'm going to have coffee and a blueberry muffin. What about you two?"

When Laurel didn't respond, Jenny said, "Coffee and muffins all around, please."

A kind of awkward silence ensued, which I eventually broke when it became obvious I would have to start the ball rolling. "It's pretty warm in here," I commented to Laurel. "Don't you want to take your coat off?"

Again she didn't answer, but she slipped out of the coat, draping it inside out over the back of the chair. She was wearing a black turtleneck sweater and black pants. Around her neck was a gold chain on which hung a striking apple-green carved jade pendant.

"Meg makes the best blueberry muffins you've ever tasted," I announced enthusiastically. "You can't pass them up."

Laurel waited for Betsy to depart, then spoke for the first time. Her voice was soft, with an edge of barely controlled hostility. "I want you to know I'm only here because of Jenny. I don't know you. I can't imagine why you wanted to talk to me."

I cleared my throat. *What am I doing playing Sherlock Holmes anyway?* I thought, as a spasm of guilt shook me. *The bumbling Inspector Clouseau is more my style.* Well, she was here and I was here. Nothing to do but go for it.

"Somehow," I began, "I've gotten . . . sort of involved in the murder of your stepmother." I didn't miss her grimace, but I wasn't sure what had caused it, the word *murder* or the word *stepmother*. Or my involvement.

"Why's that?" she asked. "Were you a friend of hers?"

The reason perhaps for the hostility. I hastened to reassure her. "I didn't know her at all." I gestured toward Franny's hunched-over figure at the counter. "I'm a friend of Franny Gold's, the woman who owns the antique shop you went to with her."

Laurel twisted around to look at Franny, who quickly brought her napkin to her face as she caught Laurel's eye in the mirror.

"Franny happened to be in Englewood the day of the

—of the accident—I mean the—day of the murder," I stumbled on. "She saw what happened and . . ." I hesitated, not certain how much I should reveal. "Well, she didn't see that much and isn't able to identify the person, but whoever did it doesn't know that and has been stalking her and—"

"You were wondering if I'm that person?"

Flustered, I said quickly, "No, no, what I meant—I just wondered if you—if you could shed any light at all on why anyone—what reason anyone would have to—I mean, because—well, Jenny told me a little of what happened when you were a child and—"

Thank God, Betsy interrupted my stammering by arriving with the coffee and a basket of warm muffins. I waited till she'd moved the little vase of flowers, set the basket down, and filled our cups. Then I started again, determined to do better. "You knew her. I thought you might have some idea who would've wanted her dead."

Laurel's soft laugh was derisive. "Anyone over whom she had any power, anyone she screwed in business, anyone who ever worked for her . . ." She paused and her voice dropped. "Anyone whose life she destroyed. It's not a small list."

My eyes darted to Jenny, who was focused on the basket of muffins. She was being very quiet, unusual for her. I took a sip of coffee and helped myself to a muffin. "Um"—I mumbled as I slathered butter all over the muffin—"what kind of business was she in?"

For some reason I didn't get, an expression of distaste flashed across Laurel's face, then was quickly gone. "She had a travel agency. It's called The Land of Oz. For people who want to live out their fantasies."

Jenny took a muffin for herself and placed one on Laurel's plate. "These look wonderful, Laur. Try one."

Laurel broke off a small piece, but she didn't eat it. She was quite slim and seemed so vulnerable I felt like doing an encore of Meg's words to me yesterday—*"Eat, bubbela, you're skin and bones"*—but I checked the impulse. Instead, I said, "Why do you think that lawyer, Mr. Grasso, said such nice things about her on TV? I know they'd had a relationship, but—"

"People always say nice things at funerals. As far as I'm concerned, she's dead and buried and she got off too easy." She reached for her coat. "There's a lot she'll never have to answer for now. Please tell your friend I'm sorry she's having problems because of what she saw. Even dead, Helena leaves a trail of victims."

Jenny reached out and grabbed her arm. "Laurel, wait. Don't leave. You could be in trouble. You did a really stupid thing meeting Helena that day. Carrie might be able to help you."

"Why should I need help?"

"Because everybody knows how you felt about Helena. You could be implicated in—what happened to her."

Laurel rose to her feet. "That's ridiculous. If I were going to kill her, I'd've done it years ago. And I'd've made sure it was slow and painful."

"Look," I said. "You don't have to talk to me. I just thought—"

Jenny's anger at her friend suddenly burst through her reserve. "Why didn't you discuss it with me or my folks before you met her? Whatever got into you? What could you possibly have thought you'd accomplish?"

You could've cut the silence that followed with

Franny's samurai sword. After a minute Laurel sank back onto her chair and in a soft voice murmured, "There were things that needed . . . to be said between us. I . . . wanted to see what I could get out of her."

"You actually thought she might confess?" Jenny gasped. "Are you crazy?"

Confess to what? I wondered. *The murder of Laurel's mother?*

"It was an opportunity I didn't think I should pass up," Laurel said. "She said . . . she wanted to get something off her chest."

"You were going to believe anything she said after she threw you out of your own home and wouldn't pay for college?"

"Why would she suddenly confess to something that could land her in jail?" I asked. "Or worse."

Laurel shifted position and avoided my eyes. "I thought maybe now that the statute of limitations has run out—"

"There's no statute of limitations on murder, if that's what you're talking about," I said. In the silence that followed I doodled on my place mat, considering Laurel's thought process. In a way, I could understand where she was coming from. A young girl whose father had married a beautiful woman too soon after the death of her mother sees the father become preoccupied with his new love. He doesn't pay attention to his daughter the way he had in the past. She becomes resentful and jealous. She wants to blame the woman on whom he'd focused his attentions, so her mind concocts a scenario in which the stepmother becomes the villain. The whole situation is compounded when the father dies and, blinded by love or weakened by illness or whatever, leaves everything to the stepmother, stupidly assuming he's leaving his child in good hands.

Of course, ever since the brothers Grimm started writing fairy tales, stepmothers have taken a bad rap, so this whole murder thing could be a figment of Laurel's imagination. I'd probably blame Eve if anything happened to my dad, although it'd be difficult to cast Eve in the role of murderer, considering that not one egg has been allowed to pass his lips since he's known her. Come to think of it, she'd be more likely to cast me in that role. But married to the health-food police or not, madly in love or not, I'd stake my life on the certitude that my father would never cut me out of his will.

"How'd your father die?"

"He had a stroke. He'd had several TIAs—ministrokes, they're called—before the big one. He took medication, but he was really pretty sick for a couple of years. Helena took over and ran the business till he died. Then she used the money to start Oz." There was a very long pause, and then she added, "She put him in a nursing home even though there was plenty of money for live-in nurses. He could've been kept home. He just wasted away in that place. And the minute she got him out of the house she started having an affair."

I had to admit, with her stepdaughter living home that took the prize for crass.

"I believe she killed my mother and married my father for his money."

I looked at Jenny, but she was carefully extracting the blueberries from her muffin and didn't return my gaze.

"I don't suppose you were ever able to come up with any proof," I said finally.

"Not of that."

"What do you mean?"

"Nothing. It's not relevant now."

"Why do you believe your father left you out of his will?"

Her voice dropped, and I had to lean forward to hear her.

"I don't know. I was young and he was very sick. Maybe she convinced him she'd take care of me. Or—"

"Or?"

"Or she forged the will."

Why wasn't I shocked? I suppose if you accept that someone has killed for money, forgery's a small thing by comparison. Of course, I didn't know how you would accomplish it unless you paid off a lot of people. Not impossible. Money buys silence. "And if you could prove it, the money would revert to you."

"I doubt it at this late date. It wasn't about the money. I don't expect I'll ever see any of that. I wanted to know the truth about what happened that night."

Maybe, but I couldn't help thinking she wasn't telling the whole truth. She was not a stupid girl. No way could she have believed Helena Forester had arranged their meeting in order to confess.

Jenny reached over and covered Laurel's hand with hers. "You were a fool. And now you've made yourself a suspect." She looked at me. "Unless—"

"Unless what?"

"Unless you'll help us. It's pretty common knowledge you were suspected of killing your husband's girlfriend. I'd hoped you'd be able to relate—"

"Oh, I can relate all right," I snapped, annoyed that my life was such an open book to the entire community. "It's exactly because I've been in a similar mess that I know how all this is going to play to the police. Look at it from their point of view." I could almost hear Ted's very reasonable voice ticking off the counts against Laurel. I mouthed what I knew he'd say. "Helena Forester's stepdaughter was totally and inexplicably cut out of her father's will in favor of Ms. Forester. Suddenly the stepdaughter, who has refused to have anything to do with her stepmother for years, is seen with her having some kind of argument. A few weeks later Helena Forester is murdered. Depending on the provisions in the father's will, on Helena's death the stepdaughter could inherit at least a portion of her father's estate." I looked straight at Laurel. "Tell me, Laurel, if you were the DA, what conclusion would you draw?"

I could hear the grandfather clock in the corner ticking away. Laurel's eyes dropped to her plate. I caught Meg and Kevin watching us through the mirror. My eyes shifted to Jenny.

"Jenny?"

"That Laurel had a real good reason to have wanted this lady dead," she replied finally.

"Exactly," I said. "Motive and opportunity."

By noon I was back home with Franny and Horty in tow, having extracted promises from both Laurel and Jenny to go back to the apartment Jenny told me she was renting on West Ninety-first Street in the city and stay there till tomorrow. Jenny would call me at the office by ten. In return I'd promised to talk to Ted before he picked Laurel up. Laurel had protested her innocence, insisting she wouldn't inherit on Helena's death; the money would go directly into Helena's estate, which surely would not be left to Laurel. She had every reason to want Helena alive. She'd never know the truth now that Helena was dead.

"She never hinted at why she wanted to see you?" I'd asked.

Laurel had hesitated, I thought, just a second too long. "She had a change of mind after we left your friend's shop. The whole thing was a frustrating waste of time."

"What did you argue about?"

"It wasn't an argument." Laurel rose to her feet. "I don't know what the lady who owns the shop told you, but the only thing Helena and I may have disagreed about that day was the value of the necklace she bought. I thought it cost too much." As she reached for her coat, her eyes fell on my doodling, and the coat slipped from her grasp. "What's that?" she whispered.

"What?"

"That—thing you drew."

I glanced down at my place mat and realized I'd drawn a reasonable facsimile of the eight-point star Franny had sketched for Ted. I grabbed her hand. "Do you recognize it?"

She was silent for a moment, then she pulled her hand away and picked up the coat. "No," she said. "For a minute I thought I'd seen something like it before, but I was mistaken. What is it?"

"What did you think it was?"

She shrugged and was halfway across the restaurant before she turned back. "Nothing. I was wrong. I have to run. I'm late for an appointment. Jenny, I'll meet you at the apartment."

And she was out of there.

* * *

The alarm people came a half hour later, and I watched nervously as they crawled around my attic laying cables and drilling holes in my walls in order to insert code panels and panic buttons. Panic buttons. If I were in a panic, would I remember to push a button? What if I were held at knife point at a place in the house where there wasn't a button? What if I were held at knife point at a place in the house where there was a button? What was I supposed to do? Say "Excuse me, would you please lower the knife so I can push my panic button?"

When the installers finished they tested the alarm, and the ensuing cacophony sent my entire menagerie into a panic. The cats, fur standing on end, started racing around the house, and Horty cowered under a chair and began outwailing the alarm. So now I know why they're called panic buttons.

Before the men left I was given two alarm codes, which, lest I forget them, I wrote down on a piece of paper. Then I attached the paper with a magnet to the refrigerator door so that the children—and also any burglar who happened along—would be sure not to miss it. One code was to get us in and out of the house, and the other was to tell the police when they showed up or called in case we screwed up and set the alarm off. I was warned to be careful not to let that happen too frequently, because the police got extremely annoyed and could hit you with a penalty charge of no less than a hundred dollars for each false alarm. Great. Between the kids and me I could envision at least one a week. Why had I ever let Ted talk me into this?

It was two-thirty by the time they left, time to pick up

Allie. I shooed Franny out the door and gingerly punched in the code. 6-4-8-2. Or was it 6-8-4-2? Damn! Too late to run back to the kitchen to check. Well, I'd find out soon enough. I rushed out, slamming the door behind me, trying to recall what the hell my police code was. 4-4-1. That was it. I waited for the siren to go off. Silence. I smiled at Franny. "By George, I think I've got it."

We'd decided to take only the fans and the parasol to show the director. The sword was a little cumbersome to tote around the halls of the high school and, speaking of panic, might cause one. I didn't intend to turn over the obi immediately. That was reserved for *my* little maid from school.

As we drove up Broadway I told Franny about my doodling and about Laurel's reaction to my mentioning the argument.

"It wasn't about the price of anything," Franny insisted. "They were angry. Even when Helena laughed . . . there was . . . I don't know, a sort of rancor behind it."

"And Laurel'd seen that star before," I said. "I'm certain of it. It scared her."

I parked the car in the school parking lot near the tennis courts. Franny and I gathered up our loot and headed for the school. Allie was waiting for us outside the principal's office.

"Mr. Creighton's in the auditorium. He got real excited when I told him about your offer, Franny. I think you've got yourself a job."

We followed Allie down the hall past several classrooms, past the cafeteria and the chemistry lab, both emitting seminoxious odors I remembered from my youth but would just as soon forget. Allie was stopped four times on the way by friends congratulating her on having been cast in the play, which entailed her introducing Franny and me and our making polite noises in response to the awkward greetings. A tall, exceptionally nice-looking boy waved to Allie from across the hall as we passed, and I noticed her blush as she kind of tossed her hair and waved back. Tossed her hair? I made a mental note to ask her about him tonight. My beautiful little girl was growing up. I'd better be prepared for the onslaught.

Mr. Creighton was a short young man in his late twenties or early thirties, with slightly thinning brown hair and a round, rather plain face lit up by a broad smile —a happy-face smile—and I liked him immediately. He pumped both Franny's and my hand enthusiastically, complimented me on Allie's "lilting" soprano, which he said was a marvelous addition to the cast, and welcomed Franny aboard as chief prop person. He oohed and aahed over the parasol and the fans, promising faithfully to treat them with the care such items warranted.

"I have a few other things you might be able to use," Franny said timidly. "And I'm sure I could find whatever else you need if you give me a list."

Mr. Creighton whipped a piece of paper out of his pocket. "I've been working on it since Allie told me about you," he said.

I peered over Franny's shoulder. He had listed several swords and daggers or cardboard facsimiles, along with bright-colored fabric for kimonos, flat straw hats, Japanese sandals, and a tea set.

"We don't have much of a budget, of course,"

Creighton continued, "so whatever you can beg, borrow, or steal to add to the set would be appreciated."

"We have lots of Asians living in Bergen County now," I suggested. "Sandals shouldn't be a problem."

"Good idea. I should've thought of that."

"And Franny has a fabulous samurai sword," Allie said excitedly.

"We didn't bring it today because it's quite dangerous in its present state. You'd have to mask the edge with tape or something, but we thought it'd be great for the Lord High Executioner."

He nearly swooned with delight. "Oh, my, yes, it sounds wonderful. You ladies must have been sent to me directly by Dionysus himself, Mrs. Burnham."

I forced a smile so as not to embarrass him or my daughter. "Allie's dad and I are divorced, so I use my maiden name now. It's Carlin," I said. "It's much easier for me since that's also my professional name, but it must be terribly confusing for you teachers. More names to remember."

A twinkle appeared in his eye. "You don't happen to sew, do you, Ms. Carlin?"

Out of the corner of my eye I caught Allie grinning. I hate sewing almost as much as I hate ironing, and my children are very well aware of it. The rule is, if anyone buys anything that's all cotton, it's their own responsibility. Under duress, I'll press an occasional wrinkled pair of pants if it really looks like Horty's slept on them, or I'll mend a seam or, once in a blue moon to save money, stitch a hem, but that's my limit. Okay, so I'll never be up for the *Good Housekeeping* award. I'll live with it. I'm sure my voice was dripping with the reluctance I was feeling. "I'm a terrible seamstress, but I guess I could manage a hem or two in a pinch if you're stuck."

"I like to sew," Franny piped up. "I'd be happy to pitch in."

I thought Mr. Creighton would hug her.

I should at least get points for bringing him this paragon, I thought grumpily. *Something on the order of a finder's fee.*

Mr. Creighton beamed at all three of us. "Well, it's been a real pleasure. A real pleasure. Thanks so much for coming by."

"Mrs. Gold is staying with us for a while," I said as we shook hands. "You can call our house if you think of anything else you need."

Allie danced her way to the car and hugged both Franny and me before we got in. "You're both terrific. You keep this up and I bet I'll get to understudy Yum-Yum."

For the first time in days Franny was smiling too. I decided those two happy faces were all the finder's fee I needed.

We managed to get inside the house without setting off the alarm. I pointed out the codes on the refrigerator door and told Allie to memorize them. She went off to vocalize, and Franny went upstairs to take a nap after refusing my offer of a snack. I suddenly realized I was starving, having eaten only half a muffin at Meg's and forgotten lunch altogether. The phone rang just as I was rummaging around in the fridge about to make myself a sandwich.

"I hear you had some interesting company for breakfast," Ted said by way of a greeting.

God, the man had spies everywhere. "It came up suddenly," I said, on the defensive. "How'd you know, anyway? You have a tail on me?"

"I assume the mysterious patient you mentioned is Jenny Margolies," he said, pointedly ignoring my inquiry.

"Mmm," I mumbled, my mouth full of leftover tuna fish.

"You eating?"

"Uh-huh."

"Well, quit stuffing your face for a minute. Is Laurel Herman there with you now?"

I swallowed fast. "With me? No. She and Jenny were going right back to Jenny's apartment in the city. It's on Ninety-first and—"

"There's no apartment rented to Jenny Margolies in New York. She's living in Tenafly with her parents."

"Not anymore, Ted. She got a job at Saatchi and Saatchi and—"

"Carrie, I just finished talking to her. When I told her you and Franny and she had all been seen coming out of Meg's Place right after Laurel left, she told me she just ran into her outside Meg's by chance, and they decided to have breakfast. When they saw you there they invited you to join them. She says she has no idea where Laurel's living. She hasn't seen her in months."

I was stunned. "But that's not true. I'll prove it to you. She left a message on my machine telling me to meet them at Meg's."

"Well, that's something. Can you go get the tape?"

My heart sank. "I erased it."

"Shit!"

"Listen, Meg and Kevin were there. Franny too. They

91

saw the whole thing. I'd told them about the meeting. They'll confirm—"

"Were they sitting with you?"

"Well, no, but—"

"Did anybody else hear you talking?"

"Uh . . . no. I deliberately chose a table where there wasn't anybody around, so we could have privacy."

"Goddammit, Carrie, why didn't you call me as soon as you got that message? You knew I wanted to talk to Laurel Herman. You knew—"

"I don't understand what happened. Jenny promised me they'd stay at the apartment. She promised she'd call me tomorrow."

"Well, she lied. There is no apartment. Obviously, she's protecting her friend."

"From what? Laurel didn't kill Helena."

His sigh sounded like it could blow the house down. "You're sure about that."

Was I? "She's so small and delicate. . . ."

"Oh, well, that certainly convinces me. How could I have overlooked the fact that only big, brawny people kill?"

"Don't be sarcastic. I just meant—"

"You meant you liked her. I guarantee you would've liked Lizzie Borden."

A very large sinking feeling was developing in the pit of my stomach. Had I helped a murderer to escape? "She couldn't have done it. It hadn't even occurred to her that she would be a suspect till I—"

"Till you disabused her of that."

I certainly had. I'd built the case against her. No wonder she'd run. I felt the tuna fish rising up.

"I'm coming over. Start making notes. I want to hear every last syllable of that conversation. Verbatim."

By the time he arrived, I'd practically worn a hole in the floor, pacing. What had gone wrong? Could it have been seeing the star? I went over in my mind everything we'd discussed earlier, trying to pinpoint what could have pushed Laurel and Jenny into the course of action they'd decided to take. I'd promised to help. I'd said I'd talk to Ted on Laurel's behalf. But before that—before that, what exactly had I said? That Laurel'd had motive and opportunity. *Brilliant, Carrie.* Ted was going to be thrilled with that little blunder.

He was.

"Jeezus Christ! You might as well have sent up a smoke signal saying, *Do not pass Go. Go directly to jail.*"

"I'm sorry," I said meekly. "Maybe it'd help if I talked to Jenny again—"

"Please, I beg of you. Stop helping me unless you want to see me walking a beat."

"Fine," I said, highly indignant. "I was going to invite you to dinner, but now—"

He got to his feet. "Can't. Got somewhere to go."

"Where?"

"Nowhere that's of any interest to you."

Suddenly I remembered. "The will. They're reading the will this afternoon, aren't they?"

No answer as he put on his jacket.

"Or have they read it already? Who inherits? Tell me!"

"I'll let you know when I know. Maybe. Where's Franny?"

"Upstairs resting. She's feeling a lot better since I've

gotten her involved with Allie's production. It's given her something else to think about besides the—besides everything that's happened. Promise you'll call me later."

"I'll think about it, Curious Georgette. Remember, keep her with you."

Is there something about me that makes the men in my life pin disparaging nomenclatures on me? With Rich it went all the way from *Kitten*, which was demeaning—although at twenty I hadn't thought so—to *Cat*, to *Nudnick*. I'd never quite figured out exactly how that last jump had come about, but it definitely hadn't boded well for our relationship. Ted had gone from *petit chou*, also demeaning—and at age forty I knew it—to *Curious Georgette*, which certainly doesn't seem to be much of an improvement. I'm not sure if being compared to a monkey is better than being compared to a cat, but it's definitely better than a nudnik. And Ted did say it with a certain degree of exasperated affection.

Suddenly, I thought of something else to be annoyed about. "How'd you know we were at Meg's this morning, anyway? Have you got someone on us?"

"On Franny, for now."

"That means on me. You just told me to keep her with me."

"Live with it."

"I'm beginning to feel like a prisoner. The house is alarmed, I've got a cop following me around—"

He leaned over and kissed me. "Two. It'll keep you honest."

I certainly didn't want to see Ted walking a beat, but almost as soon as he left, I did call Jenny. She acted as though our whole conversation this morning were a figment of my imagination.

"I didn't tell you I'd rented an apartment. I told you I was considering one on Ninety-first Street. It's too expensive. I decided against it."

"That is not what—oh, to hell with it. Why'd you lie to Lieutenant Brodsky about our meeting?"

Silence. Afraid she'd hang up, I let that go too. "Where's Laurel?"

"I have no idea."

"Jenny," I said trying to keep the annoyance out of my voice, "you agreed that she could be in serious trouble with the police. If she runs away now, she looks guilty. Why would either of you want that?"

"If she turns herself in, it'd be an easy solution for the cops. Motive and opportunity. You said it yourself. They'd probably close the case."

Why hadn't I kept my big mouth shut this morning? "I told you I'd talk to my friend. He's very fair and very thorough. He'd never—"

Her voice took on a hard edge. "Don't tell me you really believe all that crap about truth and justice triumphing in the end? What planet are you living on?"

I guess I'm as jaded as the next one about our legal system, being old enough to have observed how too often money buys justice, but where at age twenty-six was all Jenny's cynicism coming from? Maybe, I thought, from having seen Helena Forester get away with murder. More, having seen her become rich and celebrated on her ill-gotten gains.

"It would've been an easy solution for Lieutenant Brodsky to have arrested me when my husband's bimbo was killed," I protested. "He didn't do it."

"You were lucky. And he probably didn't have enough on you or he would have."

"He had the same on me as they have on Laurel. Motive and opportunity. But he—"

"Look, Carrie, I'm sorry you got dragged into this. It's really got nothing to do with you. Or with me, either, for that matter. It's not my decision."

"You mean Laurel decided to run on her own."

There was a pause. "Something like that. She feels she has a better chance of proving her innocence if she's not cooling her heels in some jail cell."

"She wouldn't be in jail. They just want to talk to her."

"Yeah, right. And how far do you suppose she'd get in her own investigation with some cop trailing her night and day?"

"Her own investigation? Are you telling me she's trying to find out who did this? My God, Jenny, how could you let her do that? Don't you see the danger she's in? These people aren't playing games. They've been stalking Franny, threatening, leaving warnings. If Laurel knows something she hasn't told us, something that could link somebody to the murder, she should tell the police and let them handle it. They're paid to put their asses on the line." I couldn't believe I was actually repeating words Ted had said to me not so very long ago, in a not so very different situation, when the shoe was uncomfortably on my foot.

Jenny was quiet for a long time. "There's nothing I can do. I don't know where she's gone. I'm sorry."

"Aren't you worried that—"

She hung up.

Great. That had accomplished a lot. Well, it had accomplished something. Number one, I'd learned, better late than never, that I should think twice before I open my big mouth. Because I had to take responsibility. It was my words or my doodling that had pushed Laurel into doing a disappearing act. Unless she really was guilty and was on the lam. Which was a genuine possibility but not one that at the moment felt right to me. Two, I'd deduced Jenny had probably tried to talk Laurel out of going into hiding and had failed. And three, I'd learned that there was a good chance Laurel was in possession of information—something she hadn't told us—something that had led her to believe she might know more about the killing than she was letting on. Which could mean a death sentence for her if she surfaced in the wrong place. On the other hand, she might not know anything and was planning to start from scratch. If I could figure out where she'd begin, maybe I could find her before she got herself killed.

Speaking of dying, I was dying of starvation. I remembered I still hadn't eaten. I opened the fridge and pulled out lettuce and mayonnaise and what remained of the tuna fish I'd been nibbling on. I mulled over what I knew while I slathered mayonnaise onto the bread. If I were Laurel, I'd begin with the present husband. But he wouldn't be available today if they were reading the will. He'd be at the lawyer's office. Which is where Ted probably was, if they really were reading the will this afternoon—and maybe where the killer was, if Helena's death was about who inherited. I covered the mayonnaise and put it back in the fridge, reached for the sprouts, added a healthy helping to my sandwich in the hope of counteracting the effects of the mayo, and took a bite. Not in the same league with Meg's crab and avocado on pita, but it would do.

I took another bite, chewed, and thought.

The charity. I needed to speak with someone involved with Helena's charity work. What if Helena had threatened to change her will and leave everything to the foundation? Who wouldn't like it? The present husband mainly, although he'd still get a third of, by all accounts, a very significant estate. Still, for some people a third of anything isn't enough. They want the whole shooting match. Helena would have inherited a third of Laurel's father's estate, but that wasn't enough. She'd wanted everything and, according to Laurel, had manipulated him or phonied the will to get it. Which brought me back to Laurel. What did I know about her? Very little, really. Where had she spent the intervening years between her father's death and the present? What did she do for a living? She'd had no money to go to college. Had she ever found a way to complete her education? Besides Jenny, who were her friends? Was there a man in her life? She was in her late twenties. Had she ever been married? Were there children? Or had she spent the past dozen years brooding, waiting for the opportunity to even the score with the woman she saw as having murdered her mother and stolen her inheritance?

I poured myself a glass of juice, picked up the second half of the sandwich, and went on a fishing expedition, giving my imagination free rein. Just suppose Laurel had a relationship with this teacher from Tenafly, the present husband. Just suppose she'd *cultivated* a relationship with him as part of her plan to get Helena. Suppose the two of them had devised a plan to do away with Helena, get married, and live on the money that was Laurel's in the first place. The perfect revenge. The piece of me that believes in an eye for an eye kind of liked it. Of course, if Laurel and Andrew Klinger didn't know each other, it would blow that theory all to hell.

I polished off the rest of my sandwich and forced my mind back to a plan of action. The foundation. That would be my first stop before work in the morning.

6

✦

"I ADMIRED HER. She was a brilliant woman, determined, hard-driving. When she set out to do something, it got done."

Were those actually tears puddling in Marlene Beasley's pale blue eyes, or was watery their natural condition? Although the room was warm, she shivered, pulling her yellow cardigan sweater close around her. The cardigan was the top half of a cashmere sweater set that matched her thinning blond hair and plaid skirt. I glanced at her feet, expecting to see bobby socks and saddle shoes, but she had chosen an updated version. Her shoes were flat-heeled brown suede. On her legs she wore opaque taupe panty hose. A single strand of pearls adorned her neck. She wore practically no makeup, only a light coral shade of lisptick, and against her pale skin her light eyebrows were almost nonexistent. Whatever sins Marlene Beasley may have committed in her fifty-odd years, vanity wasn't one of them.

Franny and I were sitting in the living room of Marlene's stately home, which was located on Walnut Street, one of the more exclusive old-money sections of Englewood, not far from what used to be Gloria Swanson's estate.

This morning, over vigorous objections, I'd stood in the doorway till my children's car pools had picked them up, then approached the garage with trepidation. I knew my Honda had been safely tucked away all night, but I couldn't shake the feeling that the stalker had somehow managed to get inside and scrawl his gross signature on my steering wheel. The steering wheel and the rest of the car were untouched. If the stalker had shown up, he'd apparently been scared off by Ted's human guard dog, although neither Franny nor I had been able to spot him on our drive from Norwood to Englewood. Either he was very good at not being detected or he'd been called off. I didn't know whether to feel nervous or relieved.

I focused my attention on the woman sitting opposite me. "She was well-liked, then, by the people she worked with?"

There was a slight hesitation. "She was a person who worked diligently for whatever cause she was involved with. There were people who resented what they saw as aggressiveness, but that's how she accomplished what she did."

"How long had you known her?"

"I've been involved with the Foundation for about three years." She glanced at me, suddenly suspicious. "What exactly is your interest in Helena?"

Too late, I realized I hadn't given that answer any thought. "Ah. Well, it has to do with, uh—" Franny saw my quandary, jumped in, and saved the day.

In her soft voice she said, "Ms. Carlin is doing an article for her professional newsletter on well-known local personalities who've made significant contributions to their communities. Talking to you was my idea, Marlene. I do hope you don't mind. I thought Helena would be an ideal subject, and the article could be a sort of posthumous tribute."

I couldn't imagine what such an article would be doing in the newsletter of the Association for Applied Psychophysiology and Biofeedback, but I couldn't come up with anything better. *She's never going to buy it*, I thought. But she did.

"How lovely. Helena would have been pleased. She did so love the limelight."

I concluded that Marlene had never heard of biofeedback. Probably thought it was something to do with biological warfare and feeding the survivors. Franny could have said I was a specialist in the science of elephant droppings and gotten the same reaction.

I overcame my peevishness and pasted a sympathetic expression onto my face. "It must be hard to lose a friend under such terrible circumstances."

"Well, I can't really say we were friends, you know— more colleagues—though, of course, I was shocked and . . . and saddened, terribly saddened by her violent demise."

Violent demise. Who talks that way, for God's sake? But I nodded politely. "Of course."

"We were thrown together a great deal because we were both, you might say, civic-minded."

It flashed through my mind that this lady also might like the limelight, but while Helena was around she'd never had a shot at it. Was that a reason to murder? Not for a sane person, and while Marlene wasn't my cup of tea, she certainly appeared sane. I dismissed the thought.

"I imagine you'll be taking over many of her duties."

She sighed as she flicked a piece of lint off her skirt. "Someone has to. I suppose I'm the logical choice. I've been doing more and more recently anyway."

"Why is that?"

Marlene's hands fluttered over her skirt, smoothing out nonexistent wrinkles.

"Helena had personal matters that took up a lot of her time. She ran a flourishing travel business, you know. She traveled quite frequently. Hong Kong, Thailand, Japan. And she was sick for weeks with the flu or something she caught on one of her trips, so I was doing a good deal of the fund-raising myself. I brought in almost all the donations for our recent benefit auction. You remember, Franny, when I was in your shop and you donated that picture? It brought three hundred dollars, by the way."

"How nice," Franny murmured.

"Everyone thought Helena was responsible for how successful the benefit was, but it was me. Not that I minded. I'm not in it for the glory."

Hallelujah and amen. Tell me another, I thought. "Still, I'm sure we all like to be appreciated when we've worked hard," I said.

She shrugged, making a superhuman effort to conceal a martyred expression. I reached into my bag and pulled out a notebook, pencil poised as though I really were preparing an article. "The Foundation—I assume it's kind of an umbrella organization. You raise money for different causes?"

"Yes, the FFH, it's called."

I made a note. "The FFH. What does that stand for?"

"The Forester Friends of Humanity. We've raised money for many worthwhile causes, not just at home but all over the world. The benefit I mentioned was for stopping the spread of AIDS among Asia's . . . ladies of the evening."

What do they do, I thought, buy a couple of tons of condoms? And doesn't charity begin at home? How about condoms for America's prostitutes?

I scribbled in my notebook, reluctant to embarrass my hostess by asking. "Is that a big problem there?" I inquired instead.

"Oh, yes. The sex trade in Japan is a flourishing industry. They have quite a different attitude about sex than we do here."

"What do you mean? They like it better?"

Franny pressed gently down on my foot.

"Well, as Helena explained it to me, Japan is a patriarchal society, and Japanese men have always had what they refer to as 'comfort women.' Today they import a lot of these women from other countries, and while we don't, of course, approve of the practice, Helena explained to me that it's our responsibility to try to protect these unfortunate women from disease."

"What countries do they come from?"

"I'm not sure. Poor countries, I imagine. The Philippines, Thailand . . ." A worried expression crossed her face. "Maybe that's not a good thing to talk about in the article. Two months ago we had a very successful benefit for underprivileged children from the inner cities. I can give you figures on how much we took in—"

"Helena never had any children of her own, did she?"

"There was a stepdaughter, but they didn't get on."

I pretended ignorance. "Oh? Why was that?"

"I don't really know. She never talked about her. I heard about her from Andy—Mr. Klinger. He told me he'd tried to bring them together but hadn't succeeded."

So Andrew Klinger did know Laurel. "Do you know him well?"

"I met him only a couple of times, but he seems very engaging and he was devoted to Helena. An extremely good-looking man. Rather young but, well, she was wealthy and still rather attractive." The last was conceded grudgingly. "Why don't you talk to him?" she continued. "Of course, now's probably not a good time. . . ."

I had a sudden thought. "You know, I never met Ms. Forester or her husband. Do you have any pictures of you and her together—perhaps with some of the other contributors or colleagues? It could accompany the article."

You never saw anyone move as fast as this lady who abjured recognition. She opened a drawer in the china cabinet and returned with a large book of photographs. Flipping through it, she paused now and again to point to a particular photo and explain which benefit it had been taken at, how much money had been raised, and for which worthy cause. Finally she removed an eight-by-ten photo that looked like one of those pictures they're always shooting of the tables at weddings and bar mitzvahs when you're trying to eat.

"This was taken at the benefit I told you about.

There's Helena with Andy, and the three Asian gentlemen next to him are associates of Helena's."

I studied the photograph. Now I knew why Helena had married Andrew Klinger. He was a strikingly handsome man with a movie-star dazzling smile and dark wavy hair, in his early thirties. His arm was around his wife's shoulder, but he was looking straight into the camera as if to say, *"Look at me, everyone. Do I belong in Hollywood, or what?"*

"I'm on her right with my husband, Ben," Marlene continued. "The dinner was twenty-five hundred dollars a plate, and every table was filled." She paused and looked at me expectantly.

I was having trouble swallowing. What do they serve people who can afford twenty-five hundred dollars for a dinner? I decided on truffles, caviar, and Lafite-Rothschild 19-whatever. "She certainly was fortunate to have you as second in command," I managed to get out. "One of the unsung heroes."

Marlene smiled warmly, gratified to have her worth acknowledged, even by such an unimportant person as I.

"The gentleman on the other side of Ben next to the pretty young woman—that's Mr. Grasso."

"Yes, I recognize him. Weren't Helena and he once . . . involved?"

"He used to be her escort at all our functions. Until he married Walawon a couple of years ago."

"Walawon. What a pretty name. May I borrow the photograph? I'll get it back to you in a few days."

"Of course. But please be careful with it."

She slid it out of its folder and handed it to me. Franny and I stood to go.

As I put on my jacket I said casually, "I'm surprised

Mr. Grasso continued to come to the events after they were both married to other people. Wasn't it a bit awkward?"

"He couldn't very well not show up. He's on the board."

I called the precinct as soon as we arrived at my office, but Ted wasn't there. He hadn't called last night despite the three messages I'd left on his machine. I was itching to know who the beneficiaries of Helena's will were, and I was relatively certain it would take a fair amount of encouragement to get him to tell me.

Franny and I had joked all the way to Piermont about the foundation's supplying condoms to prostitutes.

"Not prostitutes," I hooted. "Ladies of the evening."

"Even I don't use that term," Franny said, acknowledging her occasional slip into archaic terminology. "It does seem an odd thing for a charitable foundation to be raising money for, though."

"Well, I suppose anything that stops the spread of AIDS is worthwhile. What'd you think of Grasso's beautiful wife?"

"Rather young, but I imagine a lot easier to live with than Helena Forester would have been."

"Walawon. That isn't Japanese, is it?"

"It's Thai."

"Really? You sure?"

"I may be getting on, young woman, but I'm not in my dotage yet," Franny replied tartly. "I have learned a few things during my years in this business."

I bowed to her superior knowledge. Anyone who calls me "young woman" has to be old and extremely wise.

At the office I left her in the waiting room with note-paper, suggesting she jot down prop ideas, and began to set up for Mr. Yoshida. I asked her if she'd mind answering the phone and taking messages—not a terribly taxing occupation in that my phone isn't ringing off the hook these days. But it would give her something to do.

Mr. Yoshida arrived promptly at ten. He gave me very little history regarding the accident, only that it happened about a week ago and he'd been hit from behind. He seemed more uptight than he'd appeared on Tuesday, but some people are intimidated by having wires and electrodes attached to them. He apologized for having held Franny and me up the other evening and mentioned that he planned to stop by her shop during the coming week.

I spent about twenty minutes carefully going over how biofeedback works and how the equipment feeds back information about bodily responses. Then I explained that I'd teach him techniques to control his pain. So I was taken aback when, as I went to attach the temperature probe, he pulled his hand away as though the wire were a lit match.

"What's that for?"

"It records peripheral temperature," I explained again patiently. "People who are in pain often feel stressed and have cold hands and feet. One of the things I do is empower you to warm your hands." I picked up the EDR sensors. "These measure your stress level, sort of like a lie detector does, so I can monitor—"

"I'd rather not. Can you work without them?"

"Yes, if you'd rather, but neither one of us will get any feedback. The whole point of using the computer is so you can see what you're accomplishing." You'd think I was hooking him up to the electric chair. Not that I haven't, on occasion, had oddball reactions from other patients. One woman had to be continually reassured that it was impossible for the equipment to give her electric shocks. Another burst into tears, seeing it as some kind of test that she was bound to fail. This man seemed to be afraid that somehow I'd be able to peer into his soul and discover hidden secrets. In the end I left the sensors off and used a biofeedback stress card instead, which only required his placing his thumb on a patch in the center and waiting for the color to turn. It works kind of the way mood rings do—black for very stressed, red for somewhat stressed, green for mildly stressed, and blue for relaxed. It always impresses new patients when you can show them a nice calm blue color at the end of an exercise. Despite his impassive expression, Mr. Yoshida's stayed black.

My luck, I thought unhappily. *A new patient who obviously can use this treatment, good for at least ten or twenty sessions, and I blow it with the first.* But Mr. Yoshida surprised me. It took another ten minutes going through my book trying to find a time when our schedules coincided, but he did set up another session. As he was putting on his coat, Marlene's description of the sex industry in Japan popped into my mind, and I was tempted to ask him if he knew anything about it but decided he might find the question a little startling.

Having gone overtime with Mr. Yoshida, I was late for Hannah Tallman, my migraine patient, for which I got bawled out. Hannah is obsessive about everything, which is partly why she has migraines, but try convincing her of that. Tardiness is a pet peeve. Whenever possible I schedule her first just to avoid the hassle. As a consequence of having to calm her down before we started working, I didn't finish with Mi Sook Park, my Panic Attack, till after one. When I opened my office door, I could see Franny wasn't in the waiting room, which nearly gave me both a migraine and a panic attack, till I saw the note taped to the back of one of the chairs.

Bored to death, it read. *Went to Meg's. I'll meet you there. Franny.*

The nonringing phones must have gotten to her. I resolved to talk Meg into giving Betsy some time off and letting Franny help her out again. By the time I double-locked the door to my office, I was looking forward to a nice relaxing lunch and a glass of ice-cold Chablis. I walked through the waiting room, snagging my coat off the coatrack as I passed.

I was halfway to the door and half into my coat before it registered. I stopped dead, heart pounding like a percussion band in my ears, and turned back. There on the upper protrusion of the coatrack pole—the part that flares out above the hooks—drawn in white chalk, was a four-pointed star. The crudely sketched monkey in the center had its paws over its ears.

The stalker had been here, right here in my office! My eyes swept the room searching frantically for his hiding place. I raced around in circles like a squirrel trapped in an attic. There wasn't anyplace for a person to hide. The closet in this room is shallow, with built-in shelves full of junk, which is why I have a coatrack. Off my office there's an anteroom where Ruth-Ann works, also a bathroom, but no way could anyone have gotten in there without my seeing them. I kicked the waiting-room door shut, locked it, and sank into a chair. "Oh, God, oh,

God, calm, calmmm, I'm calmmm." Over and over I chanted my mantra, waiting for my heart to drop back from my throat into its proper place in my chest. I conquered the impulse to dash out of the office, fearing the stalker would be waiting in the elevator or in the stairwell.

How could this have happened? Franny was here most of the morning. She'd have seen anyone who didn't belong come in while I was with Mr. Yoshida. And she'd have yelled blue murder if someone had whipped out a piece of chalk and starting decorating my coatrack. She'd still have been there when Hannah came, because I'd seen her reading a magazine when I'd called Hannah in. Was she still there when Mi Sook came? Yes, because Mi Sook had mentioned asking Franny to unhook her necklace so it wouldn't interfere with the sensors I'd be attaching to her trapezius muscle. Franny had left sometime during the last three quarters of an hour, and that's when the stalker must have sneaked in here. And Ted's tail, if he was still around, wouldn't have seen him or her because he would have followed Franny when she went to Meg's.

I grabbed for the phone and called Ted. Not there. I asked for his partner. "Is Dan Murphy there?" No, Dan was with Ted. "Can you reach them? It's important." He would try. "Tell him—" I struggled to keep my voice steady. "Tell him I've—I've found another star."

The sergeant on the desk either thought he was a comedian or I was a loony.

"Like in the sky or in the movies?"

"He'll know." I clamped my mouth shut, not wanting to add "you creep," discretion being the better part of valor if I wanted Ted to get that message.

"I'll be at Meg's Place," I added and hung up before he could make a dumb reference to *Little Women*. *Not that the cretin would know Louisa May Alcott from Margaret Mitchell,* I thought spitefully. Then I called Meg's and asked for Kevin. Thank God, he was there having lunch. He came right over and walked me to the café.

"I'm sorry to be such a wimp," I said as we left the building. "It's just I've never been stalked before. I couldn't get on that elevator alone."

"That's not being a wimp. That's being smart."

"I don't know why he's stalking me," I said, trying to keep my voice from shaking and forcing myself not to keep glancing behind me. "How could I incriminate him? I know less than Franny. I didn't see anything."

"My guess is he's warning you off. You've been asking questions, talking to people who knew Helena Forester."

Hear no evil. As in hearing from people who might know something. People like Jenny and Laurel and—like Marlene Beasley. The stalker must have known where I'd been this morning!

"If I were you, Carrie, I'd back off. I hate to sound like Ted, but I know what he's going to say and he'll be right. This is police business. Leave it to them."

The way I was feeling right now, I was more than happy to oblige. There's something terrifying about being the object of a stalker. You keep looking over your shoulder, but you don't know who or what you're looking for. It's the stuff of nightmares. I was beginning to fully understand Franny's over-the-top reaction the night Meg and I had gone to her apartment.

I didn't have much appetite for lunch. I decided to forgo the wine and swallowed two cups of Meg's cure-all chamomile tea, forcing down a few bites of quiche for

Franny's sake. I didn't want to send her into a panic all over again.

"What time is Ruth-Ann coming in this afternoon?" Meg asked, keeping her tone casual.

"About three."

"Well, why don't you both stay here till then?"

"I can't, Meg. I have a two-thirty. But Franny should stay—"

Franny shocked us all by standing up and drawing herself up to her full five feet nothing inches. "I certainly will not. I am getting damned tired of this!"

My breath came out in a little whoosh. Franny had said "damn."

"This was my fault for leaving you there alone in the first place," she continued vehemently, her voice rising in volume. A few people glanced up from their plates.

"That—person is stalking you because of me. I've had enough. I am not taking it anymore. I'm not going to let you go back to that office without me. And this weekend I'm opening my shop!" She glared around the room defiantly as though ready to pummel the stalker with her handbag should he dare to show his face. Then abruptly she sat back down. We all stared at her, open-mouthed. There was a prolonged silence.

"Please excuse my language," she said in her normal hushed voice.

Everyone burst out laughing, the tension broken for the moment.

"Well, whoever it is has probably taken off by now," Meg said.

I dabbed at my mouth with my napkin and stood. "Come on, Franny," I said, feeling a hundred percent better. Well, fifty percent. "Let's go beard the lion."

Kevin rose. "I'll walk you back. I'll hang around till Ruth-Ann shows up, then I have to get to the marina."

"Appreciate it, but you don't have to stay. We'll be okay. That guy doesn't want to mess with us," I said, not wanting to be outdone in the courage department by someone nearly twice my age. "Right, Franny?"

"That's right." And squaring her shoulders like a little toy soldier, she marched to the door.

"Besides," I added, attempting to reassure myself more than anyone else, "he's already delivered his message for the day."

I dropped some bills on the table, gave Meg a hug, and the three of us left, followed by stares from curious patrons.

Ted was pulling up just as we arrived at my building. His expression was grim as he got out of the car. Catching it, Kev grinned at me. "You don't need me anymore. I'm going to take off. Good luck." He waved at Ted and headed down to the pier.

"Hi," I said.

Ted grunted some sort of reply.

"Hi, Dan," I said to his redheaded, freckle-faced partner as he got out the passenger side of the brown unmarked Chevy.

"Carrie." Dan's expression mirrored Ted's. Obviously they hadn't been having a great day. My star was the frosting on the mud cake.

"Where is it?" Ted asked, skipping the amenities.

"On my coatrack."

"You mean he was in your office while you were there?"

"It was my fault," Franny said. "I left her alone and went to Meg's. I'm so ashamed."

"Don't be silly, Franny. I wasn't in any danger. I was with a patient, and—and he was just warning me off anyway."

Ted jumped on it as we got to the elevator. "Warning you off? Warning you off what? What's he trying to stop you from doing?"

"I don't know. Probably Franny's staying with me is . . ." My voice trailed off as the elevator door opened. Franny gave me a nudge as we got on. "Tell him," she said.

I sighed. No way out of it. "We stopped off at Marlene Beasley's this morning. She used to work with Helena at the Foundation. We thought she might—"

Ted's eyes were slate gray and angry. "You took Franny with you to talk to someone who might be involved in the case?"

"Well, we were on our way here—"

"Franny's a witness. You're compromising a witness's testimony."

I was? How was I supposed to know that?

The elevator door opened. I unlocked the door to my office, and we all trooped inside and over to the coatrack in the corner.

"It's right up there, right above the—" I stopped, mouth agape. I grabbed the pole and swiveled it around. The shiny, blank surface of the pole stared back at me. The chalk sketch of the star was gone.

"I'm not crazy. It was there."

"I believe you. I wish I didn't."

"He came back," I whispered. "Why would he do that?"

"To prove to you he can get at you anytime he wants. I want dead bolts put on the doors and an alarm system installed," Ted said. "Either you agree or I'll close you down."

"You can't do that," I mumbled from deep in the recliner in my office where I'd buried myself for safety. "It's against the law." But I didn't put up too much of a fight. The guy had gotten past my not unsophisticated door lock like it was a child's toy safe. And then he'd locked it again.

"These are scare tactics," Ted went on.

"Well, I'm scared," I said weakly.

"You should be," he replied unsympathetically. "There's no reason for you to get involved in this. It's not like the thing with Meg last year."

"But Franny—"

"His messages are warnings. So long as you stop nosing around I don't think either of you is in any real danger."

I wondered if he believed that or if he was just saying it so I wouldn't freak out. "Where's your guard dog?" I asked grumpily. "Isn't he supposed to be protecting us?"

"The department can't spare a man during the day. You're just going to have to stay out of trouble." He sat in my desk chair, began fiddling with the sensors, and grinned at me. "Want me to do a little relaxation training?"

I sat bolt upright and looked at my watch. "Oh, my God, I've got a patient due in five minutes."

"You going to be okay?"

I wanted to say no. I wanted to say, *"I'm frightened and I want to go home and crawl into bed and hide under the covers."* But I knew I'd never hear the end of it, so I got to my feet and started grabbing for charts. "Ruth-Ann'll be here in a half hour. She's bringing pepper spray. I'll be fine. Go."

"Okay. See you for dinner. Give the cook a night off. I'll bring Chinese." He got to his feet, picked up his jacket, and kissed me on the nose in passing. "We'll take care of your relaxation training tonight."

He was half out the door when I remembered. "Hey, Ted?"

"Yeah?"

"Did they read the will yesterday?"

Slight pause. "Doesn't that come under the heading of nosing around?"

"Come on. I'm just curious."

"It's what curiosity did to the cat that worries me."

"I'm not going to do anything about it. They did, didn't they? Were you there?"

"Yeah."

Long pause.

I ground my teeth down to the nubs. "You going to tell me or not?"

He sighed, came back in the room, and closed the door. "It'll be in all the papers by the weekend. I might as well."

"So? Who inherits? The Foundation?"

"Nope."

I wanted to shake him. "Ted, quit it. Who'd she leave her money to?"

"You'd better sit down."

I didn't. I stamped my foot impatiently. "Ted!"

"Your little friend, Laurel Herman."

I sat. Actually, it was more like a collapse. I was dumbstruck. Had Laurel known? Had that been what the discussion was about that day? But why would Helena leave the money to Laurel? You don't heal a breach of years in one day, and Helena didn't sound to me like a woman who would have a crisis of conscience. "It doesn't make any sense."

"It gets crazier. The money is set up in trust for Laurel, but she won't see it for God knows how long."

My hands, reaching for the sensors, stilled. "What do you mean?"

"Quite a manipulator, our Helena. Under the provisions of the will, the money is set up in trust for Laurel, but the interest is split between Andrew Klinger and Donald Grasso during their lifetime. Laurel doesn't get to spend a cent till they die."

"Grasso. Why would she leave anything to Donald Grasso?"

"Beats me."

"For God's sake, he could live thirty years or more, and Andy Klinger, he could outlive Laurel."

"I imagine that was the intention."

"It's cruel. It's more cruel than if she'd left her nothing at all, which is what Laurel expected anyway. What was Grasso's reaction?"

"Shock. The will was drawn up by a now deceased colleague, who he said had never mentioned a word to him."

"You believe him?"

"No reason not to at the moment."

"So how'd he explain his sudden bonanza?"

"Figured she was compensating him for all the time and free legal services he'd donated to the Foundation over the years. He doesn't need it, of course. Said most of it will be donated to charity. Taxwise that would make sense for him."

"Just the same it seems pretty weird to me. He's married to somebody else. What woman wants another woman spending her hard-earned money?" I shook my head in amazement. I can think of a few things I'd like to leave Rich in my will, and it wouldn't be interest on anything. Crotch itch comes immediately to mind.

"So tell me. How much are we talking about?"

"Won't know till the will goes through probate and all the creditors are satisfied."

"But it's a lot."

"That's my impression."

There was a knock at the door. Time for my first Attention Deficit kid. I shook my head to clear it. "Ready in a minute, Sean," I called out.

Ted picked up his jacket. "Oh, by the way, here's another little tidbit you might want to knock around in that inquisitive noodle of yours."

"What?"

"Whoever killed Helena needn't have bothered."

"Excuse me?"

"Same as the stuff in the will, this won't be released to the press till the weekend, so keep it under your hat till then. Autopsy showed Helena had inoperable fourth-stage breast cancer. According to her doctors she'd never had a mammogram and she refused treatment of any sort. At most she had a few months. All the killer would've had to do was wait."

I brain-wave-trained four Attention Deficit kids by rote, my own brain in overdrive, my thoughts scattered. Leave it to Ted to drop a bombshell like that and then take off, leaving me ready to explode with unanswered questions. Thank God, Ruth-Ann came on time, saw my preoccupation, and filled in for me, quieting restless children and discussing their progress with anxious moms.

"What's going on?" she asked during a break between kids. "You're a million miles away."

"We had kind of an upsetting incident this morning," I replied. "You remember to bring the pepper spray?"

"In my bag. You should put it on your key ring. I'll show you how to use it."

"Thanks. Let me know what I owe you."

She nodded. "What happened?"

So I filled her in about the stalker's latest but left out the other reason for my distraction. "If you'd rather not come in till this guy is caught, I'll understand. It's not really fair to you—"

She patted her tote bag. "I can take care of myself."

I smiled at her, remembering. "You've done a pretty good job of taking care of both of us. That stalker doesn't know the trouble he's in if he shows up when you're around."

We both laughed, albeit a little nervously, and went back to work.

At five-thirty I turned seven-year-old Jake Bloom loose, handed Ruth-Ann his printout, and left her to do the honors with his mother. He'd had a pretty good session today. Ruth-Ann, a born nurturer, is really good with the little ones. Motherhood is a ways off for her, though. Her parents would like to arrange a marriage, but the new self-confident Ruth-Ann will have none of it. Sometimes, looking at my own marriage and those of a few of my now-single friends, I catch myself thinking arranged marriages aren't such a bad idea.

I shut down the computer and filed Jake's diskette.

Ruth-Ann would have to take her chances along with the rest of us. Maybe she'd be lucky.

Mindful of Ted's admonition, I didn't mention Helena's condition to Franny. Allie and Matt had both been safely delivered home by their various car pools and were delighted to learn that Ted was bringing Chinese food for dinner. Franny went off with Allie to talk *Mikado* talk, and Matt and I sat on the couch in our kitchen—family room. Emotionally spent, I lay my head back while he fiddled with the TV remote. Like every member of his sex I've ever known, he began switching from channel to channel, never pausing long enough to find out what was on.

I let my mind wander. *What woman today with half a brain has never gone for a mammogram?* I thought. This woman unquestionably had a brain. A conscience, probably not, but definitely a brain. What could she have been thinking? That she was indestructible? That nothing could touch her, that she was immune from the scourge that every other woman dreaded? Or was it something quite different, a blind spot, the ostrich-head-in-the-sand thing, a woman so egocentric she refused to confront her own mortality? Whatever had motivated her, no one would ever really know. But what could have motivated her to draw up that vindictive will? Could it have been pure spite? Or was there something else? What had that nasty exchange in Franny's shop been about?

How Helena must have loathed her stepdaughter to have tantalizingly held out the brass ring, knowing that Laurel would probably never get a chance to grab it. If Laurel's accusation had any basis in truth, there was nothing she could do about it now. So why continue the battle when you've already won? Was it because Laurel had never backed down? According to Jenny, this was a woman who would not tolerate being crossed. That accusation, spoken or unspoken, over the years must have been a thorn that festered and became as cancerous as the tumor in her breast. Maybe the will had been her final revenge.

Thinking about daughters reminded me that I'd been in such a fog lately, I'd been neglecting my own children. I reached over and patted Matt's hand.

"What's going on, sweetie?" I asked. "You and I haven't caught up in a while. How's school?"

" 'Kay."

Well, that was good. If there were a problem I'd've gotten two words.

"When's the next game? I want to make sure I don't miss it."

"Mom, it's on Saturday like always. Whatsa matter with you?"

Somebody's drawing stars and monkeys all over my things, and it's making me nuts, I wanted to say.

"Sorry, honey, I'm a little discombobulated," I mumbled instead. "Did Dad say he's coming to the field?"

"Mom, he's going to the Bahamas, remember?"

God, I'd forgotten that too. Was this stress, or is it what happens after forty?

"He's coming next week, but he's bringing the fruit-cake."

"Suzanne's really not so bad."

"It isn't Suzanne. He's got a new one."

Man, I had been out of touch. "No kidding. What happened to Suzanne?"

Matt grinned. "Dunno. She musta hit thirty."

I honestly didn't know whether to laugh or cry. I leaned over and hugged him. "It's after six. You mind if we catch the news?"

He made a face but obligingly picked up the remote and hit Channel Four.

". . . apparently by a messenger bike as he was entering the garage near his office building," Chuck Scarborough was saying. "Mr. Grasso was found wandering in a semiconscious state by a passerby. It's unclear at this time if the attack was deliberate or if the biker lost control."

I grabbed the remote from Matt and turned up the volume as I recognized from a dozen talk shows the deep blue eyes framed by horned-rimmed glasses of the tall, blondish man whose picture flashed on the screen.

"The biker has not been identified," Scarborough continued. "Donald Grasso was taken to New York Hospital for observation. His condition is unknown at present."

Ted never made it over with our dinner. Thank God for Domino's. I ordered in pizza, although to tell the truth, we were all getting sick of it. The name Donald Grasso hadn't meant anything to Matt, and I decided to wait till morning to give Franny the bad news.

Ted called just after eleven to apologize about dinner.

"I caught it on the six o'clock," I said. "I gathered you'd be busy. Was it an attack, Ted? With that lasso thing like Franny saw?"

"Nunchaku."

"What?"

"Sometimes called speedchucks. Martial-arts weapon,

couple of sticks connected by a chain. Looks kind of like a short jump rope but a helluva lot more lethal."

"How do you know that's what was used?"

"We have it."

I could hear the elation in his voice, because this might be the weapon that had killed Helena Forester.

"Is he—all right?"

"Miraculously, yeah. The perp missed him completely, and he had enough presence of mind to grab for the nunchaku as he was falling. He got off with a wrenched back and a bump on the head that had him out of it for a while. Fortunately, some instinct made him hang on to the weapon."

"Were there witnesses?"

"Typical New Yorkers, everyone was rushing to get home, no one noticed anything till he crashed into a couple of them."

"It's an NYPD case, though, isn't it? Are you—"

"The two are obviously related, and I know a lot of these guys. We may form a joint task force."

"Have you talked to him—Grasso?"

"Not yet. He's been sedated."

"Would Klinger get Grasso's share on Grasso's death?" I asked.

"No. It goes back into the trust."

So Klinger would have no motive. Laurel, on the other hand, did.

"Carrie, the reason I'm calling—"

I made a feeble attempt at humor. "Other than to hear my sexy voice, you mean?"

"Other than that. I want you to get in touch with Jenny Margolies. She has to convince the Herman girl to come in."

"I don't think she knows where she is." If I was tallying up Laurel's motives, I could be sure Ted was way ahead of me. But Laurel wouldn't have known she was going to inherit, because she wasn't at the reading of the will. Unless that had been why Helena had wanted to see her, and Laurel hadn't told us the real gist of their conversation. "You think it's Laurel, don't you?"

He didn't answer me directly. "Don't get emotionally involved, Carrie. You don't know anything about this woman."

"I just don't believe she did it."

"Based on what?"

"Instinct."

"Uh-huh. Do I have to remind you that occasionally your instinct to trust certain people has been a little off the mark?"

Ouch. That was hitting below the belt. "She's too obvious. She'd have to know she'd be the first one you guys would suspect."

"I'll tell you a little secret only we in the trade know about. Sometimes it's just that simple. What you see is what you get."

"What about the snowflake tattoo? Have you traced it?"

"Yeah. Gang logo."

"So how could that involve Laurel?" Then I remembered that Laurel had recognized the logo even though she hadn't admitted it.

"If I could talk to her I might find out. We're putting an alarm out on her. Getting Jenny Margolies to cooperate would just speed up the process," he said.

"Ted—"

"Yeah, what? I've gotta go."

I had a hard time getting the words out. "Um—if Grasso had been killed and his money had gone back into the trust—Laurel couldn't inherit unless Klinger—uh—unless—"

"Unless Klinger buys it. You got it. Work on Margolies and call me on my cell phone if she tells you anything."

I had a hard time getting to sleep. Allie was all elbows and knees, and Horty seemed to have gained twenty pounds. It was my mind chatter, though, that was the real problem. No matter which relaxation technique I tried, I couldn't turn it off, because I didn't want Laurel to be guilty. There was something about her that connected to something in me. Maybe it was her vulnerability, the way she wore that mantle of toughness like she wore that long black coat she hadn't wanted to take off, because when she did you could see that one good puff of wind would blow her over. She reminded me of Mattie that time he got in a fight over me with a couple of bullies and took a mean beating but wouldn't give up and kept flailing at his tormentors. In Laurel's case the tormentor had been Helena, and the fight had been as uneven as Mattie's. Thirteen years old when her mother died, and only fifteen or sixteen when her father was spirited away to a nursing home, a minnow against a barracuda, she hadn't stood a chance. The question was, had she finally decided to take revenge and to take back what was hers? The evidence was piling up. But somehow I just couldn't envision this hundred-plus-pound young woman with the dark eyes riding a bike, whirling that speedchuck thing, and managing to get it right even fifty percent of the time. I made up my mind to call Jenny first thing in the morning and finally fell off to sleep.

7

⋆

EVERY OTHER SUNDAY and Fridays are my car-pool days, also the day the kids see their therapist. Rich has to do the Sunday school bit on the weekends he has the children, which means he and Whoever can't laze around in bed till noon. So sometimes he'll take Friday afternoons for me, which allows me to see patients till six, and then Allie and Matt sleep at the Alpine house and he brings them back Saturday night. This weekend, though, was his Bahamas jaunt, so I'd worked through lunch and made sure not to book any patients past two-thirty.

I'd called Jenny's parents home and left four messages for her on their answering machine. My last call was to Saatchi and Saatchi, but I was told Jenny was in a meeting. I finally gave up, and by two forty-five Franny and I were parked in the high-school parking lot. We'd brought the sword and an inexpensive tea set and some fans Franny had found in the Japanese market in Edgewater. She and Meg had gone there this morning while I was at work.

"Have you ever been down there?" she asked me as, clutching our cache, we made our way through the throngs of chattering students. "It's marvelous. They have just about everything—food, dishes, even wine."

"I used to go pretty often when we lived in Alpine and I had more free time. I love sushi, and their fish is great."

"We had lunch at that pretty Japanese restaurant that looks out over the water. I'm too old to develop a taste for raw fish, though. I had tempura." She smiled at the young man who, as we walked up the steps, politely held the door open for us. "Thank you, dear. Good manners are such a joy, aren't they? Nice to see some parents are still teaching them."

"We try," I muttered.

"Who do you think we saw there?"

"No clue."

"Mr. Yoshida. Having lunch."

"Well, I guess he likes sushi too. Excuse me," I said to a bearded male who looked old enough to be a teacher. "Would you know where the community theater rehearses?"

"Probably in the auditorium. Next corridor on your left."

"Thanks."

"He was very pleasant. Mentioned again that he's going to stop by the shop soon."

"Sure you don't want to sell him the sword?"

"Let's see how Mr. Creighton feels about it first."

We arrived at the auditorium and I shoved the heavy paneled door open with my shoulder. Mr. Creighton was on the stage going over the score with a young freckle-faced pianist. We dropped our burdens onto a seat and stood listening, enjoying the lilting, clearly identifiable strains of the unique Arthur Sullivan. The piece ended, and Mr. Creighton looked up and saw us. Like a huge puppy dog, he bounded off the stage and greeted us both effusively—no licks, thank heaven, but the smile he bestowed on Franny when he saw the sword lit up his plain round face, making him seem almost handsome.

"Oh, my. Oh, my, what a beauty." Reverently, he unsheathed it and, while Franny and I watched a bit nervously, ran his finger down the blade. Then he jumped back up on the stage and began a fencing match with an invisible opponent, waving the sword in the air, Errol Flynn style. It made little whistling noises that reminded me of a guillotine.

Involuntarily, I took a couple of steps back. "Please be careful," I called. "It's very sharp."

"Oh, yes, I see, no question it could take someone's head right off," he said in delight and, with a swish, cut off the head of his unseen opponent. "Perfect—just perfect."

"Uh—you'd better keep it locked up somewhere till you do something about covering the blade."

"Of course, of course. I'll take excellent care of it. Thank you so much, ladies." Replacing the sword in its sheath, he laid it gently on the piano. Another bound took him to the edge of the stage, where he sat and addressed Franny. "I think mainly what we need to concentrate on now are the costumes. It's a simple set. I have a production crew of kids who're going to be working on it every day after school, so we're fine in that department." He eyed me balefully. "Harder to find people today willing to work on costumes."

"Are you finished casting already?" I asked quickly, determined not to let him rope me in.

"Everyone except the Mikado himself and Katisha. They're pivotal roles and the most difficult, although they're probably the most fun. I'm thinking of going outside the town and advertising in the *Record*."

"There's a lot of talent in Bergen County," I said. "You'll get dozens of responses, I'm sure."

He looked me over appraisingly. "Did Allie inherit her voice from you, Ms. Carlin? Are you a songbird?"

I had an instant vision of myself as the demonic Katisha. Long curved painted red nails, wild black wig askew, descending on the unfortunate Nanki-Poo, demanding matrimony. Talk about a release valve. Too bad the only bird I sound like is a crow. "I'm afraid I have a range of about three notes, none of which you'd care to have me inflict on an audience," I replied. "But Allie tells me your Yum-Yum is wonderful, another Sarah Brightman."

"Ah, yes, Sophie. Showed up out of the blue and blew us away. A little doll. Couldn't be more perfect for the role."

"Is she local?"

"I certainly hope so. This is community theater, after all. I wouldn't want it said I've brought in a ringer."

"I can handle the costumes," Franny joined in enthusiastically, her eyes sparkling. "Worse comes to worse we'll buy inexpensive fabric and baste them together. It'll be easier than you think."

Mr. Creighton positively beamed. "You are a treasure, Mrs. Gold, an absolute treasure."

I could see I wasn't needed, so I left the treasure safely with Mr. Creighton, happily releasing tension over a sketchbook of costume designs, and went off to collect Allie and Matt and two of his teammates. I dropped Tim and Adam off at the soccer field and headed for Closter, where the childrens' therapist had her office.

"How much longer are we going to have to see Dr. Brubaker?" Matt grumbled. "I miss practice every Friday."

"I know, sweetheart. But don't you think it's been worth it?"

"I'm sick of her. All she does is nod her head at me like it's on a spring or somethin' and ask me what I think."

"You're supposed to tell her what you're feeling," Allie said. "Not just sit there like a doofus. That's the whole point."

"That's girl stuff, blabbing all over the place. What I'm feelin' is I wanna get outta there. I don't want to go anymore, Mom."

Maybe it was time to stop the therapy. The kids seemed okay. If there were any lingering scars remaining regarding the murders of their father's playmates, time would probably take care of it. I pulled up in front of the medical building on Main Street. "We'll talk about it tonight. I'll be back at five," I told them. "Wait inside. I'll come in for you."

I was on my way to King's supermarket in Cresskill when I thought of it. I glanced at my watch. Just three-thirty. It would take five minutes to get to Tenafly High. If I was lucky and Andrew Klinger hadn't rushed out of his classroom the minute the final bell had rung, I might catch him.

I didn't think it through, didn't consider what I

wanted to ask him except that I was curious about Helena's "enemies" list that Ted had been so closemouthed about. I wondered if Klinger would tell me who was on it. I smiled as I hit the accelerator, made a right turn off Piermont onto Central, crossed the railroad tracks and headed for Columbus Drive. Curious Georgette, Ted had called me. Well, I was only going to take a look at the guy. No way could I get in trouble in front of Tenafly High talking to a teacher as though I were a concerned parent.

The closer I got to the school, the more I was looking forward to making my own assessment. I couldn't help wondering what kind of man would marry a powerhouse like Helena Forester unless it was for money. Granted, she'd had a lot of lovers over the years, so she must've had something going for her. But Klinger was young and handsome, and knowing what I did about her, even discounting Laurel's prejudice, it was difficult to believe this had been a love match. Well, he'd certainly hit the jackpot if money was what he was after. His own personal lottery. He had the interest on ten million dollars and no Helena to tell him what he could or couldn't do with it. Ten million at, say, safely, six or seven percent. My right-sided brain couldn't even compute it. But a motive for murder if ever I heard one. Of course, unless there was something I was missing—which was entirely possible—it didn't account for the attempt on Grasso.

The sun was very bright as it began its afternoon descent and briefly blinded me as I pulled up about a block from the school. I got out of the car, walked down the street, and positioned myself behind a maple tree still dressed in its red and gold glory, where I had a good view of the entrance. Twenty minutes and what seemed like a hundred kids later, I was still there, nervously wondering if he'd gone out another door and walked home. No. He lived in Englewood. He wouldn't be walking. Finally there were only eight cars left on the street: two Toyotas parked a block apart, one beat-up Ford Taurus, a Subaru, a Jeep Cherokee, an old Explorer, my '89 Honda, and a shiny black BMW sports car.

Tenafly is, by and large, an affluent community, but not many parents are about to buy their children fifty-thousand-dollar toys for them to wreck. So who owned the BMW? My money was on Andrew Klinger. I waited.

Three minutes later the door opened, and a smashing-looking guy about thirty-two or thirty-three years old,—dark wavy hair, about five ten, casually dressed in chinos and a shirt opened at the throat, jacket tossed casually over his shoulders—walked out. He was accompanied by two teenage girls who were hanging on to his every word as though he were Tom Cruise. I waited till the girls tore themselves away and jumped into the white Toyota parked two houses down. They waved and drove off. Handsome Stud headed for the BMW. I heard a beep as the remote he held in his hand released the lock. I dashed across the street and inserted myself between him and the car door.

"Mr. Klinger?"

Taken by surprise, he stopped a foot away, eyeing me warily.

"Could I talk to you a minute?"

"I'm not talking to reporters right now. I have no comment."

Oh, how I remembered that line. I'd used it on several occasions myself in an attempt to avoid pushy reporters. I almost felt sorry for him. Even as he shoved me out of his way as though I were a bag of garbage emitting noxious odors in the vicinity of his precious car, I was drawn to him by that indefinable something—call it star quality, charisma, pheromones, whatever. He had it in abundance. "I'm not a reporter," I said breathlessly. "I'm a friend of Laurel Herman's."

It just popped out. It was the only thing I could think of to say on short notice, and it stopped him dead. His hand on the door handle dropped, and his eyes darted from me to the other cars and back to me again. "Where is she? Is she here with you?"

"Uh—no. I thought you might—"

"Did she send you?"

I don't know why I said it. It was like someone else had taken over my mind—this other me, the risk-taker, Curious Georgette. "Ye-es. She's afraid the police think she's involved. She said you know who had it in for Helena."

"I told the police what I know about that."

"I realize that, but Laurel said I should ask you—"

"Are you a good friend of Laurel's?"

"I—yes." *In for a dime, in for a dollar.*

"Tell her I didn't mention the mother thing."

"You mean about Helena's . . . involvement?"

He stared at me. "You know about that?"

"Of course." *I was a close friend, wasn't I?*

"You tell Laurel to be careful." His voice dropped and he moved closer to me. "You tell her she's got to turn herself in. For her own protection." He leaned over and whispered in my ear. "I'll help her. I'll get her the best lawyers. But she's gotta tell the cops about the mo—"

There was a crash and I felt a sharp pain on the side of my head that knocked me to my knees, and something heavy fell on top of me, knocking me over on my back, and it was pressing on my chest so I couldn't get my breath. It seemed to have started raining, and the rain was like hail, stinging my skin. Dazed, I wondered why it was raining when the sun had been shining all day. But it must have been raining, because when I dragged my one free hand to my face and touched my cheek, it was wet. The pain in my head increased every time I tried to move, and my one hand pushed at the crushing weight fruitlessly. Something sharp was cutting into the back of my neck, and I tried to move my head away from whatever it was. I forced my eyes open and through a reddish haze saw Andrew Klinger lying half across me. I tried but couldn't get enough breath to say "Get off me," much less "I can't breathe," and I thought, *I'm going to die because I can't get the breath to say I can't breathe.* It seemed like hours till I heard running footsteps and voices and Klinger was finally lifted off me and I heard someone gasping noisily, and I realized it was me gulping in air as though I'd been underwater too long. And then someone said, "Who the hell is this?" and someone else lifted my head off the sharp thing and a familiar voice rasped, "Jesus Fucking Christ! Carrie!"

Sometime later I felt myself being lifted onto a gurney. I wanted to say "What happened?" but I couldn't seem to get the words out, and it went through my addled head that it would be such a clichéd thing to say and, God forbid, I didn't want to sound clichéd. I tried to sit up, but I was overcome with dizziness and my head hurt worse than ever, and I decided to hell with it. I didn't know where Ted had gone. Maybe I'd dreamed him. A uniformed cop leaned over me and asked how I was feeling, and I opened my eyes and suddenly I remembered. Through lips gone stiff I asked, "The man I was with . . ."

"Unconscious but alive," the cop said. "He was lucky. Your head deflected it. He didn't get the full impact."

Deflected what? The full impact of what? I was too exhausted to ask. *Well,* I thought groggily, *Ted'll be delighted to hear my head's good for something.* I felt an enormous sense of relief, because I knew Andrew Klinger would have been in his car on the way home if I hadn't waylaid him. Which, if he'd been killed, would have made it my fault. I let my eyes close, felt myself drifting off. When I opened them again I was in an ambulance and a paramedic was putting something over my face. I struggled to speak. "My children," I got out. "Franny—"

"What'd you say? Your kids were with you? We didn't see—Detective," he called out the back, "this lady had her kids with her."

"No, no," I mumbled. "I—they—"

And then Ted was at my side. I hadn't dreamed him after all. And he wasn't swearing at me anymore. He was holding my hand and stroking it. "What about the kids?" he said.

"What—time is it?"

He glanced at his watch.

"Four forty-five."

"Supposed to—to pick them up—at the therapist. Five o'clock. And Franny—" I stopped, out of breath, and pushed at the mask covering my nose and mouth. The paramedic lifted it off.

"Where's Franny?" Ted said, concern coloring his voice.

I swallowed and started again. "Franny—at the high-school—auditorium—with Creighton. Get her—five-fifteen."

"Okay, I'll take care of it." He started to get up.

"Wait—Ted, car pool. Six o'clock—boys at soccer field. Mattie knows—"

"**Man, these busy ladies really put us to shame,**" I **heard the** medic say from a distance. "How do they manage it all?"

And Ted's reply. "You'd think this one wouldn't have time to get herself in trouble, wouldn't you?"

I wanted to say something annihilating, but it took more effort than I could manage. Then I felt a rumble under me as the motor revved. From very far away I heard a siren. And I was gone.

When I awoke I was in a clean white bed wearing some shorty thing that wouldn't close and kept riding up if I attempted to move, which I soon discovered was too painful to be worth the effort anyway, and Ted, eyes closed, was sprawled in a chair next to the bed. A white curtain was drawn around us. A hospital, I deduced brilliantly, trying desperately to remember why I was here. I looked out the window and saw that it was dark. The only light was coming from a fluorescent tube over my head. It hurt my eyes. I tried to sit up, but a fiend from hell started banging on my head with a sledgehammer. Moaning, I fell back. I felt as though I'd been tossed around in a train wreck. Had I been in a train wreck? No, I hadn't gone anywhere. Maybe I'd been mugged. Tentatively, I reached up and very gently touched my forehead. My fingers came in contact with tape and gauze. I explored a little further, moving my hands gingerly over the rest of me, taking stock, making certain I was all in one piece. There were what felt like Band-Aids on a couple of other places on my face, one on the back of my neck, and some on my hands. I couldn't reach my legs, but every part of me was sore and stiff. What had happened? How did I get cut in so many places? I noticed a phone on the night table, reached for it, and knocked over a cup of water. Ted's eyes sprang open. One look at his face and flashes of memory, like scenes from a bad movie, began filtering back.

Klinger, I'd been talking to Andrew Klinger. He was telling me something, something about Laurel—something I should tell her. What was it? I couldn't remember. There was a crash, like something blew up or maybe a car had smashed into us or—I sank back onto the pillow and groaned loudly.

"Well, hello there," Ted said in what I construed to be a relatively friendly tone. "How're you feeling?"

If I said "terrible," maybe I could engender a little sympathy and postpone what I knew was coming.

"Kind of—terrible," I whispered, giving him a wan smile.

"Good. You deserve it."

So much for sympathy. Maybe out-and-out misery would evoke a more welcome response. "My head's killing me," I moaned.

"I can imagine. You took quite a shot."

My hand flew to my forehead. "I got *shot?*"

"I meant a blow. Your favorite artist tossed one of his metal Frisbees your way."

I started to turn my head to look at him in horror, a

move that caused such agony I stopped halfway. "I could've been killed," I gasped.

"No shit."

"God," I breathed, seriously shaken at the realization of how close I'd come to leaving my children motherless, which would practically make them orphans. I squeezed my eyes shut, trying to block out the image that flashed through my mind of them sobbing over my flower-strewn coffin. Except Jews don't strew flowers on coffins.

"To tell the truth, though, I think—as usual—you just got in the way."

I opened my eyes a slit. "You mean he—he meant it for Klinger."

"Probably, though I'm not a hundred percent sure he —or she—wouldn't have minded taking out the proverbial two birds with one stone."

She. He was thinking this was Laurel's doing. And much as I hated to contemplate the possibility, maybe he was right. The list of suspects was diminishing rapidly.

He pulled his chair closer, reached for my hand, and spoke quietly, but his eyes were shadowed with concern. "Sweetheart, you knew Klinger was a possible target. What the hell were you doing meeting him?"

"It wasn't a meeting. I mean, I didn't set it up. I just thought I'd have a talk with him."

"Why, for chrissake? What were you thinking?"

"I don't know. I was curious to see—"

He groaned. "Curious."

"Well, I was on my way to the market," I said defensively, "and it occurred to me he'd just be getting out of school, so I—"

"You had time between car pools so you thought you'd use it productively."

I withdrew my hand, annoyed. He was reprimanding me as if I were an irresponsible child. That I'd behaved like one was a possibility I found too uncomfortable to contemplate. I sighed. I was too beaten up to argue my position. Might as well be big about it. "I'm sorry," I said.

He softened. "You know what the irony of all this is? You won't marry me because I'm a cop and you're afraid—"

"I never said that," I protested.

"Shush. I'm not dense. But the bottom line is, you're the one has this damned reckless streak. You walk into situations no cop ever would without backup because you don't understand the danger. You need a keeper, not a husband. If I were smart I'd refuse to marry you."

"That's your prerogative."

"Yeah, I know. I'll give it some thought. Who wants a wife who's always out chasing killers, anyway." He leaned over and gently kissed me between Band-Aids. "Problem is, I'm stuck. You're a lunatic, but I love you."

Every so often the wariest of us succumbs to the seduction of wanting to love and be loved. Or, at least, of believing in the possibility. I returned my hand to his warm clasp. "I love you too," I whispered. And gulped.

He smiled. "I hope that wasn't your concussion talking."

"I'm not sure. Ask me tomorrow."

"Maybe what you need every so often is a good whack on the head."

"Just you try it. My boyfriend's a cop." I shifted, and the fiend from hell slugged me again. "Oh, God, my head! Where are we, anyway?"

"Englewood Hospital."

I glanced at my arm. "Why've I got bandages all over me?"

"The car window shattered. You got the fallout."

The rain. I shuddered. The wet I felt must've been my own blood. Or Klinger's. Klinger. "How's Klinger?"

"Still out."

"He going to be all right?"

"He took more of a hit than you did, but yeah, the doc thinks he'll be okay."

I hated to think what *his* head was going to feel like when he woke up. Every muscle and joint protesting, I pushed myself up to a half-sitting position. "What about Allie and Matt? Where are they?"

"Don't worry. They're home. Meg and Franny are staying with them, and I'll sleep there tonight."

"What'd you tell them? Oh, shit, I hope this didn't get in the papers. If Rich sees it—"

"He's away, remember?"

I fell back, relieved. "I forgot. First time I'm glad he's off having a high old time."

"I told the kids the truth, but they know you're okay and I told them you'll be home tomorrow."

"I have patients—"

"Meg canceled them. They're springing you from this joint tomorrow morning. She'll be picking you up."

To my embarrassment, I teared up. *I have such good friends,* I thought. And Ted—Meg was right. I didn't deserve him. I started to tell him that and choked on the words.

"Hey, hey, you're not going to go all weepy on me now, are you?"

I shook my head, sniffed, and came up with an excuse. "I think I'm weak with hunger."

Ted smiled. "You missed dinner. From the looks of what the other patients got, though, I don't think you missed much."

"You think they'd let me have some ice cream or something? I'll never make it till morning."

"See what I can do." He stretched his long legs and got to his feet. His eyes were bloodshot, and he looked rumpled and exhausted. I felt a stab of guilt. I hadn't even asked him how long he'd been sitting here watching over me, hadn't asked if he'd eaten yet. "You look tired. Did you eat?"

"Grabbed a sandwich in the cafeteria."

"Go home and get some sleep. I'll be fine."

"Let's see what I can do about the ice cream first. Got a preference?"

"Oh, yeah, like they've got forty-five flavors to choose from. I'll take whatever they'll give me."

I watched him as he pulled back the curtain and elbowed the door open, caught a brief glimpse of a uniform outside as he stopped to talk. They had a guard outside my door? I must be more important than I'd realized. Or in more danger. I glanced over at the other bed. It was empty, a circumstance for which I was eminently grateful. I didn't want to have to answer any questions about why I looked like a battered wife.

Minutes later a plump little nurse came bustling in, bearing a tray with a dish of vanilla ice cream and a tiny paper cup containing two pills. "I was told you're hungry," she said cheerfully as she wound the bed up to a sitting position. "We're always glad to hear that. How are you feeling?"

"Like somebody used me for a punching bag."

"I hear somebody kind of did." She smiled sympathetically and filled a paper cup with water. "Swallow these. They'll take the edge off. At least for a while."

I'm no stoic. Obediently, I popped the pills, polished off my ice cream, and leaned back against the pillows she'd propped up behind me. She placed a plastic buzzer in my hand.

"Here's the call button. Just press it if you need anything."

"And somebody will really come?"

She laughed. "Hopefully. So long as you don't buzz during coffee break." And rolling me back down, she turned out the light and bustled out.

A minute later Ted's head peered around the door.

"Meant to tell you, when you're back in the saddle, I've got a new patient for you."

I didn't want to think about being in a saddle. Or going to work. "Who?" I asked with a notable lack of interest.

"The man himself. Donald Grasso. Seems the fall aggravated an old back injury, and he swears the only thing that ever helped him was biofeedback. See you tomorrow, kiddo. Get a good night's sleep." He blew me a kiss and was gone.

Kiddo, I thought drowsily as the pain began to recede and my eyelids grew heavy. *Not much of an improvement, but better than Curious Georgette. Who knows, one day I might make it to Wonder Woman.*

I dreamed I was on the high-school auditorium stage dressed as the villainous Katisha. In my horrible soprano, I was singing, *"For he's going to marry Yum-Yum,"* and the audience was laughing and jeering, and they began throwing little icicles at me and the icicles became metal stars and they cut into my skin. And I ran over to Allie, who was wearing a kimono and Franny's obi and combing her hair with the decorative comb I'd bought her.

"Make them stop, Allie," I sobbed. "Tell them I'm your mother." And she went on combing and said, "You shouldn't try to sing, Mom. You have a really terrible voice." And I ran over to Franny, who was sitting on a mat and sewing a costume, and said, "Franny, I'm bleeding. Make them stop!" And she kept on sewing and said, "You can have a finger, I have dibs on the thumb." And then Donald Grasso came running out on the stage dressed as Ko-Ko, the Lord High Executioner, and he was waving the samurai sword and chasing Curious George, the monkey, and he ran out into the audience and began yelling, "Off with their heads, off with their heads!"

I woke up drenched. It was still dark, and the fiend was beating mercilessly on my head. I bore it for about ten minutes, then pressed the call button. When the nurse came in, she changed my gown and gave me a glass of water and two more of those marvelous little pills. I swallowed them greedily and slept undisturbed till they brought my unappetizing breakfast at seven.

8

✦

MEG CAME AT TEN. She was carrying a shopping bag with a change of clothes and a small bag with two of her homemade blueberry muffins and a container of coffee.

"Bless you, my child," I said as I sank my teeth into a flaky muffin. "I'll remember you in my will."

"I'd rather not discuss wills right now, if you don't mind."

"Okay," I said agreeably, munching away. I was feeling a lot better this morning. I was still stiff, but the demon had taken off to torture somebody else, probably poor Andrew, and I could move my body without its screaming in protest.

"Or maybe we should," Meg continued. "You do, after all, have two children, and with your penchant for getting yourself nearly killed about once a year, it might be a good idea to—"

"Oh, come on, Meg. How was I supposed to know it'd be dangerous to stand outside a high school and talk to a teacher?"

"Don't try to snow me. You knew the situation. Ted told me about the will and that you and he'd talked about Klinger being next on the killer's hit parade."

"Well, he didn't put it quite like that. And if he thought so, why didn't he have him watched?"

"He did, you idiot. Why do you think the guy didn't finish the job? The undercover cop took off after him."

"He did? Did he get him?" I asked, then realized of course he hadn't. Ted would have told me. The case would be closed.

"He lost him and came back to radio for help for you and Klinger." She took the empty coffee cup from me and helped me off the bed. "Don't look in the mirror."

Of course, then I had to. I dragged the bag with my clothes and cosmetics into the bathroom and stopped in front of the sink. The creature from the blue lagoon stared back at me from the mirror above it. I shrieked in horror. "They shaved my hair off!"

Meg's reflection appeared behind me. "Only a little on the side there, and I told you not to look. Let me fix it. You've got enough to cover that spot once the bandage is off." She searched through the bag and pulled out toothpaste, toothbrush, comb, and a lipstick. "Clean yourself up and put on lipstick. It'll do wonders." She began gently working the comb through the matted mess that used to be my crowning glory.

"There's more bandage than face," I mourned. "What am I supposed to wash?"

"Wash around them."

I lifted the patch just above my right eye and peered

under it. There were three neat little black stitches. "Ugh, they've sewn me up like a Thanksgiving turkey. I'm a mess." I let the patch fall back.

"You certainly are, but you'll improve."

"Ted was so sweet," I murmured as I washed whatever skin I could find. "Imagine telling me he loved me when I looked like this."

"And what did you say when he said that?"

"I got carried away. I told him I loved him too."

"Well, hallelujah. Did he faint from shock?"

I grinned, then straightened my face out. Grinning hurt. "He attributed it to my concussion."

Meg shook her head. "Poor man."

I managed to get the lipstick on my mouth despite a split lip just as Meg pushed a lock of hair from the back of my head over the shaved place. "Now you know what it's like for bald men." She laughed. "You just redistribute what you've got."

The effect actually wasn't too bad. "I've never worn bangs. I think you've given me a whole new look."

Limping back into the room, I noticed a bandage on my thigh. I stared down at it, puzzled. "How'd that happen?"

"I imagine when you fell. You tore your pants. Ted told me to bring a skirt instead of pants so it wouldn't rub."

Now, how many men would think to mention a thing like that? I sat on the bed and began to blubber. "That's it, Meg, you know. That's the problem."

"What?"

"He's *too* nice. I'm not used to—I mean, I don't quite believe him sometimes. I'm waiting to discover the big flaw."

"Oh, for God's sake."

"I'm serious. Except for being a bit of a control freak and working much too hard at a job that gives me the screaming meemies and—oh, yeah, kicking the sheets out from the bottom of the bed and tangling them all up, he hasn't got any flaws. It's not natural. He's got to be hiding something."

"You're right. I'll bet if you marry him, the very next morning you'll find out he's a transvestite with a ladies' underwear fetish."

"Don't joke."

She stopped lacing my sneaker and looked up at me. "Will you listen to yourself? Of course he has flaws. You just named three that might drive someone else to drink. But because you love him his flaws don't seem like flaws to you, just annoyances. That's what love's all about." She finished tying the other sneaker and stood up. "And the fact that you're a nutcase who keeps putting her head in the noose is obviously something he can live with and still love and want you. So what you've got isn't utopia, but it's a workable relationship. Now, let me go get the nurse so we can get out of here."

I pondered her words as I sat on the edge of the bed waiting for her to come back. Meg has such a good head. I really should pay attention. With Rich I hadn't *seen* the flaws. That was different from seeing the flaws and not minding them. Rich was charming and affectionate and smart, and I was young and in love and hadn't noticed that what he wasn't was honorable. A relationship not based on honesty isn't workable. What my very perceptive and caring friend was trying to tell me was that I had a shot at a workable relationship and I shouldn't mess it up carrying old baggage.

A few minutes later my caring and perceptive friend returned with an aide and a wheelchair.

"I don't need a wheelchair," I protested.

"It's policy till you get out the door," Meg said. "Don't you remember from when you had babies? The hospital doesn't want any lawsuits."

"It makes me feel helpless," I mumbled, but I sat down gratefully and let myself be pushed. I knew it was going to be some time before I felt like jogging again. Not, speaking honestly, that I ever do feel much like jogging.

The cop who'd been guarding me was gone from outside my door, off to get a well-deserved day's sleep, I hoped. We were in the lobby at the cashier's window filling out the final paperwork when I looked up and saw Jenny Margolies at the information desk. I nudged Meg. "Oh, my gosh, there's Jenny. Run over there and grab her. Don't let her get away."

"What am I supposed to do? Wrestle her to the floor?"

"Maybe you won't have to," I hissed. "Maybe she heard about the accident and is coming to see me."

Meg picked up the shopping bag. "Okay, but this is the last time. And I'm calling Ted on my cell phone and telling him she's here. Your involvement is over. I promised him I'd stop you from doing anything stupid, if I had to tie you up and chain you to—"

"Meg, wait!"

She stopped. "What now?"

"Turn around. I don't want her to see us."

"What? You just told me—"

"I'll bet she's come to see Klinger, not me," I whispered excitedly. "We need to follow her. We need to hear what she says to him."

"He's unconscious, you crazy person!"

"Maybe not anymore. Wait till she gets on the elevator and then go over to the desk and ask what floor he's on."

"Ted'll kill us."

"No, he won't. He'll kiss our feet. 'Cause I'm sure she knows where Laurel is, and if Klinger's conscious I'll just bet she's going to tell him."

Meg was back two minutes later.

"I have his room number, but he's only allowed one visitor at a time and it has to be family."

"What're you talking about? Jenny's not family."

"She passed herself off as his sister. So that's it. Let's go home."

She dropped the shopping bag with my ruined clothes onto my lap and started to push me past the flower shop toward the door.

"Meg, wait. It's Jenny we want to talk to. We can at least go up there and—"

"No. I promised Ted." She kept on pushing.

I started to climb out of the chair, but Meg increased the pace and I fell back. What a way to treat a wheelchair-bound patient!

"Listen to me, Meg," I cried, hanging on to the arms for dear life. "This is an opportunity we can't miss. Jenny's our—" I half-turned to look at her over my shoulder and almost fell out of the chair onto the highly polished and very hard floor. Then I felt the wheelchair hesitate under me and pressed my advantage. "She's our only link to Laurel. Ted wouldn't want us to pass this up. If she disappears—"

The wheelchair slowed.

"Why don't we just go up to the floor and wait for her to finish with Klinger?" I inquired reasonably when I'd caught my breath. "What could it hurt? Nothing could possibly happen. We don't have to go into his room. I'm sure Ted has a uniform posted outside his door, anyway."

The wheelchair stopped.

"We don't have visitors' passes. They won't let us up."

"So long as I'm in this chair no one's going to stop us. And if they do I'll just say I forgot something."

"Got it all figured out, haven't you?" Meg grumbled. But she turned the chair around and we headed for the elevator bank.

I was right. The wheelchair was an open-sesame. No one questioned us when we passed the nurses' desk. Except, of course, the uniform when we arrived outside Room 721.

"Sorry, you can't go in there," he said.

I smiled sweetly. "I was with Mr. Klinger when he was injured. I'm leaving the hospital today and I just wanted to say hello, see how he's doing."

"He's conscious, but I have strict orders. No visitors. Sorry. I just sent his sister away."

My heartbeat accelerated. Klinger was conscious! "Jenny?" I asked innocently, glancing up at Meg. "Oh, I'd hate to have missed her. Did you notice where she went?"

"I think to the lounge. You might want to take a look there."

"Thanks. Please tell Andrew I was asking for him," I called as Meg swung my chair around and, dodging in and out of the walking wounded toting their IVs, we zipped down the wide corridor.

But the lounge was empty.

"Damn, damn, damn!"

"Wait a minute." Meg disappeared around the corner, was back a minute later. "She's on the phone."

I was out of the wheelchair and standing outside the phone booth before Meg could stop me. No way was Jenny going to escape me this time. She saw me just as she hung up and turned to open the door. I blocked her path.

"We're going to talk," I hissed through the crack. "If you won't talk to me, I'll tell the cop outside Klinger's room that you're not his sister and might have had malicious intent when you tried to see him. He'll hold you till they send someone to take you to the precinct."

The threat would've scared the hell out of me, but Jenny was a tough cookie. Partially my fault. I'd given her too many positive affirmations. She pulled a small address book out of her handbag.

"Well?" I said impatiently. "You coming out?"

"I'm calling my attorney," she said coolly. "I don't care for threats." And she clapped the folding door closed, almost taking my poor beat-up hand with it. I watched in frustration as she dropped change into the phone.

I threw Meg a desperate look. "She acts like I'm the independent counsel out to drag her before the grand jury."

Meg handed me her cell phone. "She's bluffing. Let her see you making good on your threat. Call Ted." Then loudly she said, "I'll go get Security."

Jenny looked up at her words and suddenly hung up the phone. She pushed the door open. "What is it you want from me? I don't know why you think this is any of your business anyway."

I was outraged. "Take a look at me. I'm not quite as gorgeous as I was the last time we saw each other, am I?

153

If it wasn't my business before, it sure as hell is now. I could've been killed. I'm being stalked. I don't know why or by whom, but I have a strong gut feeling you do."

The tough expression on her face disintegrated and she brushed past me, walked into the lounge, and sank into a chair. "I don't know who's behind all this," she said softly.

Meg and I pulled up chairs opposite her. "But you know what it's about. And you know where Laurel is."

"I know where she was."

"Who were you talking to just now?"

"My mother," she said in a small voice. "Laurel was staying with us, but she's gone now."

"There's an alarm out on her. You've been obstructing justice, are you aware of that?" I said angrily. "That's an indictable offense." *God*, I thought. *I'm even beginning to sound like the independent counsel.* I made a conscious effort to soften my tone. "Look, Jenny, if you know anything you'd better tell me. If it's not important I won't mention to Lieutenant Brodsky that your family was hiding Laurel. But you have to tell me what you know even if it means betraying a friend. After all, no matter what happened in the past, if Laurel committed murder—"

"She didn't."

"How do you know that?"

"I know her. It's not in her."

Not good enough. "We don't always know people as well as we think we do," I said. "How close are you to her?"

"She lived with us after Helena threw her out. We were like sisters. My dad put her through college. I know she didn't do it."

"Well, who did? Who else wanted Helena and Grasso dead?"

"Don't forget Andrew Klinger," Meg interposed. "Somebody wanted him dead as well."

"Well, that just proves it wasn't Laurel. She may have hated Helena and Donald, but—"

"Wait a minute. She hated Grasso? Why?"

Jenny's face colored. Her eyes dropped to her lap. "I need a tissue," she said and began digging around in her purse.

"Why'd she hate Grasso, Jenny?"

"She . . . always thought he was the one who helped Helena forge her father's will," she mumbled after a moment.

I was rendered speechless by a fit of coughing. When I could speak I said, "*The* Donald Grasso who got battered wife Marta Gonzales off death row, Donald Grasso, defender of Josiah Hansen who helped his pain-racked, terminally ill wife die peacefully? Donald Grasso, TV icon? Is she nuts?" My next thought was that maybe she was. Maybe all that hatred had come to a boil and had finally exploded.

Jenny shrugged. "She was a kid, and he was Helena's lover. It seemed logical at the time."

"Well, if she still believes that, maybe she *is* doing this. Maybe she's cracked up, Jenny, and she needs help. You have to help us find her."

"She didn't have anything against Andrew other than that she thought he'd sold himself," she murmured, but there was less certainty in her voice.

Unless she knew about the will. Was it possible Laurel didn't know about the will? Suddenly I Andrew's words to me: ". . . *she's gotta tell the cops about the mo*—" Money? Mother? *Monkey?*

A white-haired man leaning heavily on a walker made his halting way into the lounge and stood several feet away from us, gazing longingly out the window. I dropped my voice.

"How well did Laurel and Andrew know each other?"

"They went to high school together, but I don't think they saw much of each other after that. And certainly not after Andrew married Helena."

Andrew had married Helena. If Laurel's mind were unbalanced, it wasn't beyond the realm of possibility that Andrew would have also become a target. I struggled to keep my face impassive, not wanting Jenny to read my thoughts. "Why'd you want to talk to him?"

"When I heard about the attack"—she reached over and touched my arm on one of the few un–Band-Aided patches—"I felt awful that you were hurt, by the way."

"Yeah, thanks. Go on."

"Well, my folks and I figured he would have been at the reading of the will, so he'd know who benefited if something happened to him. We figure it has to be somebody from the Foundation, because that's probably where the money would go."

She was either an awfully good actress or she really didn't know about the trust for Laurel and the way the will had been set up.

"Did Laurel tell you what the argument with Helena was about?"

Jenny shook her head. "She only said she was onto something that would bring Helena and her cohorts down, but it would put us in danger if she told us."

"Helena's dead! How much more down can she get?"

A doctor in a white lab coat ushered a middle-age couple through the archway and over to a couch in the corner, where they sat and began talking in hushed tones.

"What does Laurel do for a living?" Meg asked.

Jenny hesitated, then said, "She's been working at a health-food store in Nyack."

"Is she married? Is there a man in her life?"

"Not that I'm aware of." She picked up her briefcase and got to her feet. "Sorry, I've got to get back to the office. I can't afford to take time off. It's a new job."

I grabbed her arm. "Listen to me, Jenny. Laurel's got to turn herself in. She—"

"Well, well, Ms. Margolies. Just the person I was hoping to see."

I jumped guiltily as I looked up and saw Ted's tall frame looming in the doorway.

"And Ms. Carlin," he added. "Just the person I was hoping not to."

I rose and limped over to the wheelchair. "Meg and I were just leaving when we ran into Jenny," I said, plopping myself into it.

"You were leaving the fourth floor by way of the seventh?"

"I came up to see how Andrew was doing," I mumbled, annoyed that he was making me feel defensive. "We were going to call and tell you Jenny was here."

"Well, I saved you the trouble," he drawled. "I was informed Klinger was conscious, so I thought I'd drop by."

We all stared at him, waiting for him to go on. His gaze swiveled to Jenny. "Fortuitous that you're here,

Ms. Margolies. Saves me the trouble of having you picked up."

"I really have to get back to work," Jenny began.

"I'll write you a note. Let's talk." His voice was pleasant, but I know him. I saw that all too familiar "don't give me any crap" look in his eyes.

"What did Andrew tell you?" I asked without thinking. Then I realized that Ted would be looking for inconsistencies from Jenny so, of course, he wouldn't say anything. But he surprised me.

"Mr. Klinger has had a slight lapse of memory. He remembers nothing of the accident or of the events preceding it. Or so he insists."

"Well, that's a bummer," I said to Meg as we turned onto County Road. "You think he's telling the truth?"

"Andrew? No way of knowing. Ted sounded skeptical."

"Yeah. I keep trying to remember what it was exactly Andrew said to me about Laurel. Something about money. Tell her to tell them about the money or her mother, something like that."

"Who did he want her to tell?"

I thought hard. "I think he said the cops."

"That doesn't make much sense."

"It does because he wanted her to turn herself in."

"Why would he tell you to tell her anything?"

I stared out the window, fixed my gaze on the rows of houses with their nicely groomed lawns flashing by. I was reminded my leaves needed raking. "I . . . uh . . . kind of indicated Laurel had sent me."

Meg heaved an audible sigh. "Why doesn't that surprise me?"

"The crash happened right after that, so everything's really kind of a blur. He must've said "mother," because what money could he have been talking about? He couldn't've meant the money from the trust because the cops already know about that."

We drove along in silence. Meg broke it as we braked at the light at Union Street in Cresskill.

"Your fridge is starting to look like Mother Hubbard's cupboard. Wanna stop at King's? I'll cook you up a chicken casserole for dinner before I leave."

But my mind wasn't on dinner.

"You know who we need to talk to?"

The light changed, and Meg made a left and pulled into King's lot. "Nobody who has anything to do with this case, I hope."

"The people in the health-food store. If Laurel's been working there for a while, she must have made some friends. Maybe she's staying with one of them. Somebody must know something."

"Excuse me." Meg opened the car door and snagged a nearby basket that was rolling by. "When you say *we* have to talk to these people, are you using the pronoun in the royal sense or are you planning to involve me in this insane pursuit, which I just promised your lord and master I'd keep you from undertaking?"

I grinned. "He's not my lord and master, so I can do as I please."

Meg rolled her eyes heavenward.

"I answer to no one," I announced firmly as I pushed myself to a standing position, "which, now that I think of it, is probably one of the reasons I've been keeping it that way."

Meg shook her head. "You pay a price for that freedom, my dear friend. I hope it's worth it."

When we got home from King's, the kids and Horty were standing at the door waiting for us. Allie put her arms around me. "You okay, Mom?"

"I'm fine. Just a little bruised."

"They cut off your hair, and you're all puffy and purple," Honest Abe Matt said. "You look awful."

"She doesn't either. I like you with bangs. They're very becoming. You want to go upstairs and lie down?"

I leaned over to pet Horty, who was sniffing at my Band-Aids with more than a little interest, and managed to refrain from yelling "ouch" as I straightened up too quickly. The thought of climbing stairs, when muscles I wasn't aware I had were unpleasantly making their presence known, did not appeal to me at the moment. "No, honey, I think I'll just stay in the family room and watch Meg cook dinner."

Not to be outdone, Matt slid an arm around my waist. "You can lean on me, Mom. I'm stronger than Allie."

The dampness of his hair and the pungent boy aroma rising off his skin reminded me he must've just gotten home from his soccer game.

"Sorry I missed the game, Mattie. Who won?"

He flashed a grin. "Who do you think?"

"How could I have doubted it? The Green team, of course. Congratulations." I dropped a kiss on the top of his head.

We arrived in the kitchen—family room, and I eased

myself down onto the couch and allowed Matt to lift my legs up onto it while Allie solicitously placed a pillow behind my head. Lucie jumped on my stomach, which was the only part of me that could safely be jumped on without my screaming like a torture-chamber victim, and started to purr. Moments like this make childbirth and car pooling and that god-awful music they listen to all worth it. "My goodness, I don't know when I've had so much pampering," I joked. "How long do you suppose I can count on it?"

"Do not question, just enjoy it." Meg laughed, putting the bag of groceries down on the counter. "Who wants to peel carrots?"

They both actually chorused, "I will." They say every cloud has a silver lining, and I'd definitely found the one in this storm cloud. I smiled contentedly and closed my eyes.

"Oh, I almost forgot," Matt said. "Grandpa called."

My eyes flew open. Good-bye, contentment. "You didn't tell him I was in the hospital, did you?"

Matt looked sheepish. "Well, um . . . yeah, I—"

"He did, the big dweeb," Allie said in disgust.

I groaned. I couldn't help it. Because I believe I'd rather face that star-flinging stalker again than listen to my stepmother Eve's long-suffering tirade about my propensity for bringing disaster down on the family and worrying my poor father into an early grave.

As if conjured up by my thoughts, the phone rang. Everyone looked at me expectantly.

"Well, someone answer it," I said grouchily. "I'll have to face the music sooner or later."

Matt got there first. "Hullo?"

I could hear the overage sweater girl's high-pitched

voice even though the receiver was pressed against Matt's ear.

"Mattie, dear, it's Auntie Eve. Grandpa's making himself sick over your mom, so I had to call. Is she home from the hospital yet?"

"Uh . . . well, she . . ." Matt looked at me helplessly.

I nodded my head and struggled to a sitting position, dumping poor Lucie unceremoniously onto the floor. He stalked off, an act he does so dramatically I think he must practice when no one's looking. "Give it to me," I muttered.

Mattie handed me the phone, and I put on my best "everything couldn't be better" voice. "Hi, Eve."

"Carrie. My God, Carrie." Unspoken was, *"How could you put us through this again?"*

"Listen," I said brightly. "I'm absolutely fine. Much ado about nothing. You know how they are in hospitals. They keep you overnight just to cover their own rear ends. How's Dad?"

"He *was* fine. Please tell me what exactly happened."

I rolled my eyes. The kids started to giggle.

"I was standing in front of the school talking to a teacher who has a fancy new BMW. Some maniac decided to take out the window. Got a few cuts and bruises, that's all." Nobody, not even my kids, could accuse me of lying. I just wasn't telling the whole truth and nothing but the truth.

Big sigh on the other end of the line. "You do always seem to be in the wrong place at the wrong time."

"Well," I said cheerfully. "All's well that ends well. Can I speak to Dad?"

Another enormous sigh. "Just a minute. And for

heaven's sake, try and stay out of trouble. All that running around you do—"

"Oh, hush up, Eve." My father's voice. "Give me the phone. Hi, sweetheart. You really okay?"

How I love this voice. Ever since I can remember, just hearing it makes me feel safe. I swallowed. "I'm fine, Dad. And being so well taken care of by your two grandchildren, you wouldn't believe it."

"Well, good. Ted with you too?"

"Not at the moment. He's working. Meg and another friend, Franny, are here, though." I glanced around. Where was Franny? "How're you doing?"

"Pretty good for an old man."

"You're not old. You'll never be old."

"Why don't you and the kids come on up to Worcester for a visit? I miss you. Haven't seen those two monkeys since Allie's Bat Mitzvah."

I shuddered at the word *monkeys*. If I never saw another one, it'd be okay with me. "If I can take some time off work, maybe we'll come during Christmas vacation."

I could hear Eve in the background making noises about the cost of the phone call, so I let Allie and Matt talk to their grandfather and then we hung up.

Don't get me wrong. I don't dislike Eve. She just wouldn't be my first choice for stepmother. Then again, who am I to criticize anyone's taste? And so long as she makes my dad happy, which seems to be the case, that's all I care about.

Allie went off to practice her scales, and Matt and his friend Jeff shut themselves in Matt's room with some new computer software Jeff had brought over.

"Where's Franny?" I asked Meg when we were alone.

"She convinced Ted to let her open her shop today. She'll come back here to sleep tonight."

"Was that a good idea? I'm surprised Ted—"

"She's a grown woman and she needs to make a living. He couldn't stop her. I asked Kev to take a run over a couple of times, and I'll look in on her when I go back to the café this afternoon."

I watched as Meg expertly chopped an onion into tiny, symmetrical pieces, marveling at her precision. My chopped onions are never neat and symmetrical. But then neither is my life. "Who's running the café?" I asked.

"Betsy. Now, why don't you take a nap while I concentrate on the coq au vin?"

I yawned. I was tired, but I couldn't stop the wheels from turning.

"What're you doing tomorrow, Meg?" I asked casually.

"You mean after I make brunch for about forty people?"

"Yeah."

"I was hoping to do something normal, like fool around with my husband before he takes off for Key West."

"Oh. Well, God knows you're entitled."

The hand pouring the wine into the pot paused. "Why do you ask? What's going on in that devious mind of yours?"

"Nothing. Nothing."

"Bull. Tell Aunty Meg or I'll pour this magnificent concoction down the garbage disposal and you'll have to eat pizza again for dinner."

That did it. I pushed myself up with my hands. It's amazing what happens to your pelvic muscles after the deadweight of a hundred and seventy pounds of man has been lying across them for fifteen or twenty minutes. I felt kind of like I did after my C-sections.

"I'd like to take a ride up to Nyack. Everything's open on Sunday."

"You may run into Rambo. Remember, he's having a nice little chat with Jenny as we speak."

"I need some dried flowers from Petals and Lace. I can't help it if it just happens to be on South Broadway, where Born of Earth and Nirvana are."

"How do you know she works at either of those?"

"I haven't been to Nyack in a while, but unless there's a new health-food store I don't know about, it has to be one or the other." I stretched and immediately regretted it. "Besides, I really need some Rescue Remedy for my pain and stress. I guess we'll just have to make a side trip."

9

*

HAVING DISTRIBUTED THE KIDS after Sunday school and lunch to the homes of various friends, I pulled up in front of Meg's Place at precisely one o'clock. My aches and pains had diminished to an acceptable level, and the bruises had faded to an unattractive jaundice color. I'd removed the bandage from my head and covered the stitches with my stylish new bangs. Except for a few Band-Aids, I felt I was presentable enough in my neat skirt and blouse not to send anyone into anaphylactic shock at the sight of me.

I double-parked, beeped, and Meg jumped into the car.

"What've you got in this thing?" she remarked as she removed my purse from the passenger seat and dropped it onto the floor.

"I don't know. Wallet, notebook, checkbook, cosmetics, pepper spray. Adds up."

"Feels like you're packing a forty-four."

"Don't I wish."

We inched our way through the maze of Sunday traffic up the block to look in on Franny. I'd dropped her off at about ten this morning, and people were already standing outside her shop waiting for her to open. It was a bright, crisp fall day, and the town was teeming with tourists. Everything normal. No sense of lurking danger. Franny's shop was packed. She saw us through the window and waved. We waved back and took off.

"She's been missed," I said to Meg. "They were lined up outside her door this morning like she was giving things away."

"She's an institution. Everyone loves her."

"Everyone but the stalker."

"She'll be okay. She's developed a clientele, people who stop by every weekend. They'll be in and out of there all day."

"Nobody's lining up outside my door," I complained.

Meg patted my hand. "Everyone loves you too, and if push comes to shove you can wait on tables at Meg's Place."

"If things don't improve in my office, I may have to."

"Or you could marry Ted."

"Back off," I muttered.

"Or you could live together," she went on blithely. "Either way it would help financially."

"What're you—on his payroll?"

"Just offering solutions."

"Some solution. How would it look to my kids if we did something like that?"

"This is the nineties. And they're not babies. They know what's what."

"How would it look to my dad and Eve?"

"Well, you've got me there," she replied, her voice drenched with sarcasm. "I don't know where I got the idea, but I was under the impression you were of age."

"Can we drop it, please?"

"Happy to."

We rode in companionable silence, enjoying the panoramic view of the Tappan Zee sprawling across the Hudson like a giant arm connecting us to the body of Westchester and ultimately to the heart, New York City. Strangely, notwithstanding the aversion to water I'd acquired during the events of the past couple of years, this river and this bridge have a euphoric effect on me. New York's skyline seen from any of the towns bordering the Hudson is magical. And I've probably come to associate this area with some of the better times in my life, the times with Ted and the kids, and even with Rich years ago. We had watched the armada of big sailing ships floating up the river from around here, and Ted and I hiked and picnicked last summer along its shores. Polluted though it may be, the Hudson is home.

Despite the road being one-lane and narrow, I always drive to Nyack through the villages of Rockleigh and Grandview rather than taking Route 9W or the Palisades Parkway. The scenery is worth the extra few minutes. There are times I've thought about moving back to the city when the kids are grown if I could afford it, but I'm trapped by an obsessive craving for the scent and sight of forsythia and cherry blossoms in the spring and autumn's kaleidoscopic changing of the guard. Rich used to say you have to give something to get something. Of course, I'd never suspected he was planning to give me to get Erica, which just proves you should listen very hard and make an effort to read between the lines when your mate tells you something.

I turned up Voorhis and onto South Broadway and started searching for a parking place in front of one of the arts-and-crafts-filled Victorian houses lining the street. Just beyond the library I found one.

Mindful that Ted could show up at any time, we hurried the couple of blocks to Born of Earth. As we walked in the door, our senses were assailed by the tangy smells of spices and herbs. I squelched an overwhelming urge to wander the aisles and check out the vitamins and minerals and the herbal remedies and skin creams and all manner of exotic health foods that lined the shelves.

"Isn't this wonderful? It's enough to make you want to bathe in aromatic oils and become a vegetarian," I whispered to Meg.

"Take a look at the prices. You'll change your mind."

I picked up a small jar of oil guaranteed to reduce facial swelling and discoloration—right up my alley at this particular moment—but speedily replaced it as my eyes lit on the $23.99 price tag.

"Guess I'll let nature take its course," I said regretfully.

A young woman wearing dangling earrings, denim overalls, and a tie-dyed shirt approached us.

"Can I help you?"

"I need some Bach's Rescue Remedy."

She reached behind me and took a tiny bottle off the shelf. "Anything else?"

"Um—oh, yeah, last time I was in Laurel told me you'd be getting in some Thai spices. Did they arrive yet?"

She looked puzzled. "We always have Thai spices. What did you want?"

"Uh . . ."

Meg to the rescue. "Lemongrass seasoning."

The girl disappeared and returned with a small bottle. "This what you mean?"

Meg took the bottle and examined it. "You know, this looks very nice. I'll take it."

Well, if we didn't find Laurel, at least the trip wouldn't be a total loss. I could guarantee lemongrass chicken on Meg's menu by next week. "Where is Laurel, by the way?" I slipped the question casually into the conversation as I dropped a ten and a one onto the counter. "Is she off on Sundays?"

"Who?"

"Laurel Herman."

"I don't know her."

"Doesn't she work here?"

"Not since I've been here, and that's about eight months."

"Oh, she must be at Nirvana, then."

"Or Jasmania," the girl said, handing me my twenty cents' change.

"Where's that?"

"Health-food place over on Main. Just down the street from The Coven. Only been open about a year."

"How much did you pay for that ridiculously minuscule bottle?" Meg asked when we were out on the street.

"Nine ninety-five plus tax."

"Jesus. What did you say it rescues you from?"

"Stress."

"I thought you do that."

"I do it for other people. This does it for me."

She shook her head. "What's wrong with this picture?"

"I only use it during extremely stressful times," I said defensively. "Being stalked and attacked does seem to fall into that category."

"In your case, that's par for the course."

"Funny."

We waited for the light at the corner and started up the incline, passing Ichi Riki, which is Nyack's one Japanese restaurant. The streets were as packed with people as the streets of Piermont are on weekends. Nyack is larger and overflows with all kinds of interesting shops and eating places and galleries, all guaranteed to please the eye and palate and lighten the wallet.

"I could go for some sushi."

"Stop thinking about your stomach. You want to find Laurel or not?"

Grumpily, I muttered assent, and we stopped before a tiny hole-in-the-wall store with an orange and blue sign over the door that read JASMANIA. Painted across the top of the window were bright, decorative astrological signs. Scattered throughout were candles of all sizes, shapes, and colors, and books and posters peddling everything for fitness from products to activate your brain and help you lose weight to courses in meditation, t'ai chi, and shiatsu. All promised a healthier body and mind and a more serene life.

"Hey, this'd be a great place for you to advertise," Meg said. "You might pick up some clients. It'll be our secret that your body's beat up and the word *serenity* isn't in your vocabulary."

"Oh, it's in my vocabulary. I just don't seem able to incorporate it into my life."

The shop, dimly lit and empty, was long and narrow. The pungent smell of scented candles or incense or both invaded our senses. I'm not an expert on the difference. Behind the counter an upper-thirtyish muscle-bound guy with a small tattoo on his upper left arm and hair pulled back in a ponytail glanced up as we came in. At the back of an aisle displaying herbal teas and organic spices and vegetables, I noticed the shadow of a girl with long dark hair, who was stacking what looked like spice jars on a shelf. For a minute I thought it was Laurel, but a beam of light caught her face as she bent down and I saw that she was very young and Asian.

Having blown my wad at Born of Earth, I walked directly to the counter and came right to the point.

"Hi," I said. "We're looking for Laurel Herman. Does she work here?"

The man visibly stiffened. "Not right now. Can I help you with something?"

"I have to talk to her. Could you give me her address?"

"Sorry. We don't give out personal information." He turned his back on me and began taking greeting cards from a box and arranging them in a display rack.

I put all the urgency I could manage into my voice. "It's terribly important that I find her right away."

Suspicion saturated his voice. "Why?"

I hesitated. If this was Laurel's boss and I told him she was in trouble, he might fire her. I didn't want that to happen, but I needed to make him understand the gravity of my mission. "I have some information for her about an inheritance," I said.

"You can give me the info and I'll pass it on when I hear from her."

I was losing patience. "Could you please just tell me where she is?"

He stopped stacking and turned to look at me. "She's on vacation."

"Where?"

His tone was hostile. "Who wants to know?"

He wasn't the only one feeling hostile. "The police, for one," I snapped.

"You a cop?"

"I'm a friend."

"No kidding. So am I. How come I don't know you?"

"I'm . . . a new friend. Look, if you know where she is and you care what happens to her, you'll tell me how I can reach her."

He bent over and started removing bottles of vitamins from a carton at his feet. "Sorry."

"Listen, you—"

I felt the pressure of Meg's foot on mine. People are always stepping on my foot to shut me up. Next time I go out, I'm wearing Matt's soccer cleats.

"Mike," she said in a conciliatory manner, glancing at his name tag, "we should've introduced ourselves when we came in. I'm Meg Reilly, and this firebrand here is Carrie Carlin." She leaned slightly toward him, zapping him with a dazzling smile. "I respect that you're trying to protect Laurel, but—"

That was as far as she got, because the door opened and two Arab women wearing long black robes and face veils came charging in, and without a glance our way, they headed straight up the spice aisle toward the girl with the long black hair. It flashed through my mind that I'd never seen veiled women here in Nyack, only in the city and not very often there. I was about to comment on it when suddenly Mike vaulted over the counter.

"Hey," he called, dashing after them. "Hold it—"

Meg and I stood frozen in shock as we heard what sounded like a cabinet falling over. There was a scuffle followed by a high-pitched scream and the sound of breaking glass. I started down the aisle and saw that Mike had one of the women pinned against the wall and the other one was dragging the girl by one arm toward the door. Jars and bottles came crashing to the floor as another shelf went over. The girl was struggling with her attacker and trying vainly to save herself by grabbing at whatever she could get her hands on. It skidded through my mind that I'd been wrong about her nationality, she must be from some Arab country, a runaway from a restrictive culture. Her kidnapper had her half out the door when, without considering the consequences, Meg and I went into action. I went for the woman, swinging my purse, pummeling her around the shoulders and face. Out of the corner of my eye I saw Meg snatch a couple of cans off a shelf and aim for the gut.

"Look out, Carrie," she yelled.

I dodged out of the way as the cans connected. The woman grunted and doubled over, losing her grip on the girl's arm. I grabbed a piece of robe and the veil fell away from her face. Before it had quite registered that the face under the veil wasn't a woman's, he'd shoved me aside, dashed out the door, and jumped into a waiting black sedan. The other very male pant leg aimed a kick at Mike that sent him to his knees, then he shouted something in a language I didn't understand and, grabbing the girl around the waist, began dragging her into the street. She was screaming and kicking, people were stopping, stunned, not reacting yet, when I felt myself pushed aside and a voice I recognized shouted, "Let her go!"

I turned. Laurel Herman had a gun pointed straight at the man's heart.

He got the message, dropped the girl as though she'd turned radioactive, and jumped into the car. It roared off, tires screeching.

Meg and I ran out to the street. The girl lay curled up in a ball, sobbing, Laurel and Mike hovering over her. A crowd started to form around them.

"I got the license plate," Meg yelled.

"Somebody call 911," I got out.

"No." Mike turned to the crowed. "No police, please. It's a family matter."

I looked at Laurel. "What's going on?"

The girl threw an imploring look at me. "No police. Please," she pleaded.

"It's a family matter," Mike repeated. "She's okay. No need to bring the cops into it." He leaned over, gently lifted her to her feet, and, placing a comforting arm around her shoulder, led her back into the shop. The excitement having passed, the crowd began to disperse muttering among themselves.

Laurel turned to Meg and me. "Thanks a lot for your help," she said. "I'm really sorry about this. Those two sons of bitches were her brothers. They don't want her working here."

"They didn't behave like any brothers I've ever known," I said. "They tried to kidnap her, and they weren't at all brotherly about it."

She shrugged. "It's a different culture. Please, I'm sorry. I have to close up. The place is a mess and she's upset. I have to go to her."

I planted myself firmly in her path. "No way, José. You're not disappearing on me again. The police are looking for you."

"I'm sorry. I can't talk to them right now."

"You have no choice."

Her hand shifted downward and I saw the gun that she'd shoved into her waistband. "Yes," she said quietly, "I do."

My heart jumped into my throat, but I stood my ground. Even if she was the killer—and from the look in her eyes, I was beginning to think she was—I didn't believe she'd shoot me right here in front of all these Sunday shoppers. "If you're innocent you have nothing to worry about."

"And the meek shall inherit the earth. Right." She turned to go inside.

"Come on, Carrie," Meg whispered in my ear. "We'll call Ted."

"Who's the girl, Laurel? Tell us that at least. Is what just happened here connected in some way to Helena Forester's murder?"

She hesitated at the door.

I pressed my advantage. "Come on, you owe us an explanation. They'd have gotten the girl if it weren't for Meg and me."

She turned back. "You have to promise to give me time. If I tell you anything, you have to promise not to call the cops."

"You can't do that, Carrie," Meg whispered warningly.

Talk about killing, I was dead meat if I let Laurel get away from Ted a second time. "Let's hear what she has to say," I muttered.

"Do I have your word?"

Time is a relative thing. "Okay," I said.

"She hasn't got mine," Meg hissed in my ear as we followed her into the shop.

If Laurel was the killer, I was thinking we were doing a pretty stupid thing walking into this shop. There were three of them and only two of us, and one of them had a gun. From Laurel's expression when she'd faced down the kidnapper, I was pretty certain she was capable of using it. What had become of the gentle girl I'd met at Meg's café only a few days ago? I left the door open. Laurel moved behind me and closed it.

"Sit down," she said.

I brushed some cans off a large carton and sat. Meg perched beside me.

"I'm working with an international organization," Laurel began.

Oh, for chrissake, I thought uneasily. I'd bought into that kind of bullshit once before, much to my regret. "Not the FBI?" I inquired sweetly.

There was no mirth in her smile. "You don't have to believe me. All you have to know is that this girl was brought into the U.S. illegally under false pretenses to service corporate executives."

"What do you mean 'service'?"

Her face hardened. "I mean fuck. I mean she was supposed to be a sex slave."

"Oh, come on," I said, annoyed that she'd think we'd be so naive as to buy that. "That doesn't happen in this country."

"Really. Would you care to tell her that?"

"Who brought her here?" Meg asked. "How are you involved?"

Laurel hoisted herself up onto the counter and regarded us thoughtfully, considering, I suppose, how much to reveal to us. I was considering how much of it would be the truth.

"You probably know my mother was half Thai. A couple of years ago, I was visiting her family there when I heard about a teenager who was promised a job in a factory in Japan by Helena Forester herself. She was from a very poor family, rural, lots of children—the job sounded like a way out to her. When she got there she was held captive in a bar, forced to have sex many times a day to work off the fare owed to Helena's travel agency. She killed herself. She was fifteen. I was with her mother when she threw herself across the casket at the funeral."

It was a shocking story, and as Marlene Beasley's words came back to me, I did believe it. It took my breath away.

"From that day on, I've been working with an organization called the Alliance Against Trafficking in Women. It's based here in New York. You can check."

"Are you telling us that Helena brought this girl here?"

She nodded. "She thought she was going to work for Helena as a domestic."

"And governments condone this?" Meg asked.

"There're people who are trying to stop it. But we live in a global economy, businessmen travel, and sex is big business everywhere. In Japan the sex-tour industry is very big. Has been for years."

"But . . . Helena's foundation raises money to protect Asian prostitutes from AIDS," I said. "Her associate told me—"

"She wanted the girls healthy. No matter how many

child virgins are imported from Thailand or the Philippines, they're only virgins—and therefore disease-free—once."

"You had a personal vendetta, though," Meg said. "Your interest in this isn't purely altruistic."

"You bet. I hated Helena Forester, and I jumped on the opportunity to expose her. But I hated her because I knew who she was. I'd lived with her. She was totally amoral. Everything she ever did in her life bore that out. But I didn't kill her."

"So who did?" I asked.

"I don't know yet. I do know, in order to run the sex tours, Helena needed the protection of a yakuza family. You pay big bucks for that kind of protection. My guess is she may have shortchanged them or tried to cut them out. There're other possibilities, of course. Families of children whose lives she's ruined—"

"These men, then, who tried to kidnap this girl—they weren't her brothers? They were—what did you call them—yakuza?"

Laurel nodded. "Gangsters—Japanese mafia. To them she's a commodity they bought and paid for. Like cocaine."

"But then who assaulted Grasso and Andrew Klinger? They're not connected with the travel agency, are they?" Meg asked.

Laurel shrugged. "Andrew found out about the agency's sponsoring sex tours on one of their trips, but he swore to me he wasn't involved. He actually helped this girl escape. He may be greedy, but he's not totally without conscience. As for Grasso, he'd be crazy to be part of it at this stage of his career."

I was thinking about the throwing stars and the tattoo. If someone knew about Helena's connection to the yakuza and wanted to make the killings look gang-related—someone who had something to gain by the deaths of Grasso and Klinger—someone who had an old ax to grind—

Suddenly I wanted to get out of there, fast. I got to my feet. "Well, I think you should be working with the police on this. You have information they need, and you certainly can't protect this girl forever."

"I'd be happy to work with them if you can guarantee they won't throw me in jail."

I was inching toward the door. Meg took the hint and followed me. "I told you the other day I'd talk to Lieutenant Brodsky."

Laurel read my mind but made no move to stop us.

"And I'd get about as far with him as I have with you, right? I had motive and opportunity. Isn't that what you're still thinking, Carrie?"

I paused with my hand on the door handle. "It doesn't matter what I think. What matters is stopping whoever's doing this, and if it isn't you, you'd better get yourself and that girl out of the line of fire."

She slid down off the counter. "That's exactly what I intend to do."

10
✴

MONDAY ROLLED AROUND and I found myself too busy to concentrate on anything but work. Having children and a job tends to get in the way of the investigative process.

Soon after Meg and I had left Jasmania, we'd found a phone and called Ted, but neither he nor Dan were at the precinct. I'd left an urgent message, telling him where Laurel was, but he hadn't called back. I was in a quandary because by now I'd become suspicious of Laurel. If she herself wasn't the killer, it was possible she'd hired a hit man from this gang.

The phone was ringing as I entered my office.

"Biofeedback Center."

"Well, I see you made the papers again."

My head, which had been pain-free for a whole day, started aching. "How were the Bahamas, Rich?"

"Peaceful, which obviously is a state completely unfamiliar to you."

"Why, thank you, I'm feeling much better. Thoughtful of you to ask."

I was surprised when he sounded embarrassed. "Sorry. You okay?"

"I'll live. How're you?"

"Boiled like a lobster. Fell asleep in the sun."

Poor baby.

"You want to bring me up to date?" he asked.

Keep it on a need-to-know basis, Carrie, I warned myself. "It wasn't personal. I just happened to be in the wrong place at the wrong time."

"What else is new?"

I bit back a biting retort. "So there's nothing to tell."

"You sure? Didn't it have something to do with this case your cop friend is working on?"

Damn. How would he know this was Ted's case? "Hold on a minute, Rich. My patient just walked in. Be right with you, Mr. Yoshida," I called out to no one. I counted to ten, then got back on the phone. "My patient's here. Let me call you back. I'll explain everything later. Nothing to worry about."

"I wasn't worried. Just wanted to be sure the kids are okay."

"They're fine."

"They'd better be."

I slammed down the receiver. "I hope your entire skin peels off in slow, agonizing strips, you self-centered bastard."

I flipped on the computer and was pulling Mr. Yoshida's chart when the phone rang again. I let the machine get it.

"Carrie, you there?"

I grabbed it. "Ted? Hi. You get my message?"

"Yeah, I called in. I sent someone to pick her up."

"I hope she was still there. Where've you been?"

"In the bowels of New York. How're you feeling?"

Warmth flooded me. *To hell with you, Rich Burnham,* I thought. "I'm a lot better. How're you?"

"Exhausted. Not much sleep. I've been following some leads."

"Yeah? What'd you find out?"

"More than I ever wanted to know about Gurentai yakuza."

"Laurel mentioned yakuza."

"She did? Tell me."

I brought him up to date, going to great lengths to omit the attempted kidnapping and my part in stopping it. I figured that could wait till he'd mellowed out over a glass or two of wine. "Do we really turn a blind eye to the importing of young girls as sex slaves in this country?"

"A lot of us are in the trenches trying to stop it. But does it go on? Sure. It's one of the fastest-growing criminal enterprises in the world today. Child prostitution in this country is out of hand, and believe me, ninety-five percent of those little girls and boys are homegrown."

"It's horrible."

"Sweetheart, the human animal is not one of God's best efforts. I'm gonna grab some shut-eye. Let's go out for dinner. I've been living on greasy burgers and egg rolls."

"I can't leave Franny and the kids alone."

"I'll put a man on the house."

"You got it, then."

"See you about seven."

Mr. Yoshida came at nine. As he sat in the recliner, I saw him staring at my bruises, but he quickly looked away when he caught my eye. I sighed. I was going to have to come up with a reasonable explanation for every patient.

"I'm not a battered woman," I joked. "I was in a little accident." That would suffice for those who hadn't picked up the story in the papers or on TV.

He nodded. "I am sorry. Are you all right?"

"A little sore, but basically fine. You'll have to forgive me if I move a little slowly today, though."

I was pleased to find him more relaxed and somewhat responsive this morning. He even agreed to allow me to attach the temperature probe to his finger. I figured we'd work up to the other sensors one session at a time. We did a progressive muscle-relaxation exercise, and while I wasn't able to monitor his progress in the usual way, he did manage to raise his temperature two degrees and the stress card turned red, which was an improvement over last week's black. He even surprised me, when I was making small talk at the end of the session about Franny's search for props for *The Mikado*, by offering to pick up sandals and those little one-toed socks worn with them.

"Oh, we didn't think about those," I said. "Thanks. It's awfully nice of you to go to the trouble."

"Happy to do it," he said. "I'm in New York very often. There are places to get things quite cheap."

He made an appointment for next Monday, and just

as he was leaving I remembered my conversation with Ted. "Oh, Mr. Yoshida, have you ever heard of"—I wrinkled my brow, trying to recall Ted's exact words— "Gurentai yakuza? I know the yakuza are the equivalent of our mafia, but I've never heard the term *Gurentai*."

He was half out the door when he turned back.

"Where did you hear it?"

"I . . . read something in the paper . . ."

His body relaxed. "Not people you would want to get involved with, believe me. It's an outlaw group even from the yakuza families, who generally kill only their own. The Gurentai have no boundaries—no, as you say, honor among thieves. They kill for hire."

I wanted to ask more, but he'd closed the door behind him.

The phone rang as I was resetting the computer to brain-wave train my next patients.

"Ms. Carlin?" a deep voice inquired.

"Yes."

"Donald Grasso here."

I hadn't dreamed Ted's words to me in the hospital!

"Yes, hello. How can I help you?"

"I'm told you're a miracle-worker, and I need a miracle."

I laughed nervously. "I don't think I'm quite that good. You have to consider the source of your information."

"I have great faith in the judgment of Lieutenant Brodsky. Would you be able to see me today?"

I grabbed my book. It'd be tight, but my next two patients were adult ADDS who didn't need to be talked to or taped. I could finish them by eleven-forty. If I ate lunch in the office instead of going to Meg's place I could fit him in. I wasn't going to pass up the opportunity.

"Can you be here by eleven forty-five?"

The Voice resonated warmly in my ear. "I'll leave my office by eleven. I'm most grateful." God, the man oozed charm even over the phone.

He oozed charm in person as well. He arrived promptly at eleven-forty, accompanied by a burly male secretary/bodyguard who looked like an Irish prizefighter. The prizefighter sat in the reception area with a cell phone and a notepad and managed to look industrious before Grasso and I'd even gotten out of the room.

I'd seen Donald Grasso on television on several occasions, but I wasn't quite prepared for his commanding presence. I guessed him to be somewhere in his mid-forties, with hair that was almost totally prematurely white, not blond as I'd thought when I saw him on TV. He wasn't as tall as I'd thought either, maybe just under six feet, and he walked with a slight limp, which only seemed to make him more attractive. He was dressed impeccably in a charcoal-gray pin-striped suit and a white shirt, and his tie looked as though it had been painted by Chagall. He spoke in a deep, slow drawl with just a tiny hint of Southern. But it was the startling Paul Newman blue eyes behind those horn-rimmed glasses that riveted me. I thought he'd make a terrific hypnotist and told him so. He laughed and joked about what a great advantage that would be in front of a jury.

"How long have you had back problems?" I asked after I'd hooked him up and we'd done a brief relaxation exercise.

"I took a bullet in the back several years ago. It didn't go near the spine, thank God, but every so often my coccyx kicks up, and I've found that the glove anesthesia you people do helps me. The fall I took last week seems to have aggravated the condition."

I was stuck on the part about the bullet. "How'd you get shot?" I inquired, in the same cool, professional manner I use when I ask my patients about automobile accidents.

"Got caught in one of those third-world uprisings. What happened to me last week, though, was far more unsettling."

Despite the calm manner in which he spoke, his EDR was off the screen. This man was practiced at covering his feelings. To bastardize a very old hair-color commercial, only his biofeedback therapist would know for sure. I adjusted the numbers. Fifty-seven. A long way from the optimal two but, under the circumstances, understandable.

"Would you like to talk about it before we go on?"

"You mean why it was more frightening than getting shot?"

"If you'd like to tell me."

"When I got shot it was random. Last week someone was trying to kill me. Me personally."

"Do you have any idea who or why?" I held my breath.

He let out a sigh. "You don't get where I have without making enemies. Besides which, when you're in the public eye, the crazies come out of the woodwork with all kinds of imaginary grievances."

"I suppose that's true," I said. "Still, if you could narrow your list down to someone who also hated Helena Forester, it'd probably help."

"I guess I'll have to leave that to your friend, the detective, and the antique lady. His job—finding out who has a reason to want Helena Forester, Andrew Klinger, and me dead."

Was he inferring that he believed Laurel was guilty?

"I hear he's very good," he added.

"Oh, yes. Not much gets by him. He has a way of piece by piece putting the puzzle together."

He smiled and closed his eyes. "I'm impressed. I'll rely on you to keep me up to date on his progress."

Listening to the man, I found myself doubting Laurel's story. I wanted to ask him if she'd ever accused him to his face of helping Helena forge her father's will, but I could hardly do that. Instead, I decided to see if I could get a clearer picture of the woman a lot of people had disliked and someone had hated enough to kill.

"I heard you on TV talking about Ms. Forester. I'd like to express my condolences."

His eyes opened. "Thank you. We were good friends."

"Did you know about her illness?"

"No. She wouldn't have wanted anyone to know. That's how she was."

"I guess she was a pretty complicated woman," I ventured. "I've heard so many different stories about her."

He knew what I was talking about. He laughed. "You've been talking to her stepdaughter, I'll bet. You got the wicked-stepmother version."

"Well . . ."

"People like Helena aren't always appreciated. She

liked to win. It's what made her successful and why her foundation was able to accomplish what it did."

"Still," I said, leading the conversation in the direction I wanted it to go, "it's too bad she died before they were able to resolve their differences. I think Laurel was hoping—"

"Laurel has problems. She never gave Helena a chance. I myself tried to get those two together, but . . ." He shook his head. "No use."

"Oh, then it was you who set up the meeting a few weeks ago."

He paused. "No. I'd given up on any reconciliation between those two."

I couldn't ask any more questions without sounding unprofessionally nosy, so I went on to helping him create numbness in his hand, which he then transferred to the painful area in his back. He was a responsive patient, having done this before, and by the time we finished he was feeling better.

"A miracle," he said. "Lieutenant Brodsky is a lucky man."

"I'll be sure and tell him you said so."

"Perhaps you and he would join me for dinner one evening—if he ever takes any time off, that is."

I couldn't believe my ears. Dinner with the rich and famous. "I'd enjoy that," I said offhandedly, as though we received these invitations every day. "Would you like to come for reinforcement later in the week?"

"I'll have my secretary call. Thanks so much, Ms. Carlin. I'll recommend you to all my friends."

Who knows, I thought. *With Grasso in my corner, I might become one of the rich and famous myself.*

* * *

Ted's alarm people were due at four, so I'd given Ruth-Ann and two of my Attention Deficit kids the afternoon off, knowing I'd be able to see patients only till they arrived. I worked straight through, managing to take a fifteen-minute break for lunch. When I left at twelve-forty to pick up a sandwich at the grocery store, I double-locked the door, uncomfortably aware that it wouldn't stop the stalker should he be inclined to leave me another message. But I was back within ten minutes, so he had a very small window of time in which to practice his art. Which is not to say I didn't keep my pepper spray clutched tightly in the palm of my hand as I reentered the building.

The alarm people—four brawny, relatively brainy (I hoped) men—came on time and stampeded through my office, causing much consternation as they snaked their cables and wires around my expensive equipment. To give credit where credit's due, they tolerated my anxious cries of "oh, God, be careful" and "that's very delicate equipment" with amazing aplomb. They were finished by a little after five-thirty, leaving me the leery possessor of a new set of alarm codes. I figured it was only a matter of time before I confused them with the ones for the house and had the police of both towns living high on my fines.

I was fifteen minutes early getting to the high school to pick up Allie, so I parked the car and went inside, hoping to catch some of the rehearsal. I heard Allie's clear soprano ringing out as I walked down the corridor. I hesitated just outside the auditorium, concerned my presence might embarrass her or make her nervous.

When I finally opened the door a crack and peered in, I saw that she was singing a duet with the young man I'd seen wave to her in the hall last week. Mr. Creighton was at the piano, and a few of the cast members were scattered around the auditorium. The boy had a good tenor voice, and a thrill of pride shot through me as I stood listening. There was something about them, call it chemistry or star quality (being a mother, I naturally prefer the latter), that kept everyone watching.

If I never accomplish anything else in my life, I thought, *I can be proud of how my kids are turning out. I did it right.*

Wait a few years before you start patting yourself on the back, warned that pesky little voice inside my head that keeps me honest. *The job's not finished.*

I crept into the darkened theater and slipped into a seat in the back row. I hadn't heard Allie practice this particular song—didn't recall that Pitti-Sing had a duet with Nanki-Poo. Then I realized that she was singing one of Yum-Yum's songs, because the lyrics were about how Nanki-Poo would never kiss her, *"like this and this and this,"* and between each *"this"* the boy kissed Allie on her cheek, which turned redder with every one. Mr. Creighton must have given her the understudy job. Allie would be walking on air.

The song finished to enthusiastic applause from the onlookers. Allie giggled and the boy gave an elaborate bow before they walked over to the piano to talk to Mr. Creighton. I got up and made my way to the stage.

"Hi, everybody," I said brightly. "That sounded very nice. I haven't heard you sing that song, Allie."

"It's not my song," she said. "I was just helping Alec out 'cause Sophie didn't show up today."

Not wanting to jump to any wrong conclusions, I

said, "Oh, that was Yum-Yum's duet. No wonder I haven't heard it. What happened to Sophie?"

"I don't know," Mr. Creighton said glumly. "She didn't call. I've telephoned her twice, but there's no answer."

"Maybe she just forgot."

"We've only got three weeks to rehearse," he grumbled. "Forgetting isn't an acceptable excuse."

"No, of course not."

"Mom, this is Alec Roderick. He's playing Nanki-Poo."

"Hello, Alec." I smiled at the tall, dark-haired young man, definitely more Prince Charming than Frog, who was the cause of Allie's rosy complexion. "You sounded great just now. You must be excited—getting to play the romantic lead."

"I am," he replied. "And Allie did a terrific job on such short notice. She's a much better sight reader than I am."

I wasn't sure if it was his words or the way he was looking at her that made Allie's complexion turn at least two shades deeper. I pretended not to notice and focused on Mr. Creighton. "I have a patient who's going to try to get us sandals and those one-toed socks they wear with them."

Mr. Creighton bounced off the piano bench and grabbed me enthusiastically by the shoulders. I tried not to scream in agony.

"Ms. Carlin, I am forever in your debt. One-toed socks. I would never have thought of them." Suddenly aware of the tortured expression on my face, he dropped his arms and stepped back, eyeing my bruises in alarm. "My goodness, whatever happened to you?"

I took a deep breath and stretched my lips in what I

hoped was a smile. "I'm afraid I got in the way of some broken glass."

"Oh, I'm so sorry. You should be home resting."

A couple of clichés came to mind. *No rest for the weary. A woman's work is never done.* But I thought that sounded too self-pitying, so I opted for martyr to impress my daughter and the young man whose adoring gaze she was returning. "It looks worse than it is. I'm fine, really."

"Well, you're a special lady. Not only have you brought me that wizard with the needle, Franny Gold, but you have produced a golden child with a golden voice who may well end up being our Yum-Yum."

My eyes flashed to my daughter, whose face had lit up like the sky on Independence Day, but she managed to control herself and say the right thing.

"Oh, Mr. Creighton, I'm sure Sophie will be here on Wednesday. Maybe she misunderstood about today being the first rehearsal. I mean, her English isn't really all that good."

"That's true," he said. "I'll call her again tonight."

"Where does she live?" I asked. "Maybe she's sick. If it isn't too far, I'd be happy to stop by her house."

"I only have a phone number," Mr. Creighton said forlornly. "I'll just have to keep trying her."

"Well, go easy on her," I said, picking up Allie's books and jacket from one of the seats. "We all mess up sometimes. I once forgot an appointment with the superintendent of schools."

"Mom, you didn't."

"Honest. Why do you think I'm no longer on the PTA board? I've been banished for life."

We were half out the door when Mr. Creighton came running after us, Franny's sword in hand. "Ms. Carlin, would you mind holding on to this until technical rehearsal? The powers that be don't want me keeping it here at school."

"Even with tape on the blade?" I asked.

"They're afraid some kid will get his hands on it during rehearsals and do something stupid. Everyone worries about school violence these days."

"Maybe it'd be better not to use it," I said, gingerly taking the sword from him. "Cardboard would probably work as well."

"Well, we'll see. I'll let you know what the final decision is."

Allie practically skipped all the way to the car. I hated to bring her down, but I thought it might be wise to interject a little reality into her euphoria in order to prevent a crash later on.

"Allie," I said as I unlocked the trunk and laid the sword inside, "Sophie's only missed one rehearsal. Maybe you shouldn't get your hopes up too high."

"I know that. But I'm definitely her understudy, and Alec's noticed me now."

"I could certainly see that, although if my memory serves me correctly, he noticed you the other day."

"Yeah, because we were both in the cast, but it's different when you get to work together."

I glanced over at her sparkling eyes, the glow in her cheeks, and had a sudden flashback to a production of *A Midsummer Night's Dream* my first year of college. I'd captured the role of Hermia and fallen madly in love with the strikingly handsome senior who played Demetrius. He was the darling of the theater department, and I was a lowly freshman. I remember what it felt like, that moment when I realized he was as attracted to me as I to him. I reached over and patted Allie's hand, two females bonding. She smiled at me gratefully.

"You don't think I'm awful to wish Sophie doesn't show up on Wednesday, do you?"

"Of course not, but don't count on it. Why would she have tried out if she wasn't serious about being in the show?"

"I don't know. I told you, she's strange."

"You should try to make her feel more comfortable. You know a lot of people in the cast, and if you're going to understudy her, it'd be good to be friends."

"It's hard. She's much older than I am."

"Yeah, you said. How old is she?"

"I don't know. Eighteen, nineteen."

I nodded my head. "Yeah, that sure is old."

"You know what I mean."

I laughed. "And how old is the sexy Nanki-Poo?"

There was loud silence accompanied by a lot of squirming under the passenger seat belt. "Seventeen," she mumbled.

"I see. That's a lot older than you are, isn't it?"

More silence. I let it drop, more aware than ever that the little voice in my head was dead on. I had a long way to go before I could pat myself on the back about a job well done.

It was six-thirty before we got home, because I'd had to go back to Piermont to get Franny and then swing by Jeff's house to pick up Matt. Over the weekend I'd made arrangements to have Matt's soccer car pool drop him at a friend's every day except Friday. Fortunately, my fellow drivers have busy enough lives that no one asked unwanted questions. Of course, there're two ways to look at that, which gave me pause as I thought about it. Maybe no one cared enough to ask questions. Partly my fault. I'd been so busy and preoccupied since we moved to Norwood, I hadn't taken the time to make friends with the locals. I promised myself that as soon as these murders were solved, I'd have some people over to dinner. Think of the dinner-table conversation when I remarked that Donald Grasso had invited Ted and me to dinner. No one would be able to say my parties were dull.

I sent the kids to take Horty for some exercise, warning them to stay on our block, while Franny and I started dinner. By the time Ted arrived at seven, my new bangs were stuck to my forehead and I felt grubbier than Horty looked when he returned from his run. I managed to slip the chicken pot pie into the oven, yell to Franny to let Ted in, and dash upstairs. Twenty minutes later I'd showered, changed into a long black skirt and my favorite black and blue sweater, plastered makeup on my black and blue marks, and combed my now clean hair into my new hairstyle. It was a record for me (the incentive being that quiet romantic dinner), and the results were better than expected. Ted's whistle of approval made me glad I'd gotten upstairs before he rang the doorbell.

"Put the alarm on as soon as we leave," I instructed Allie and Matt, who were already stuffing their faces with pot pie. "And do your homework. Don't give Franny any trouble."

"They're angels," Franny said, patting Matt's cheek. "Why would they give me trouble?"

I kissed the tops of two heads. "Okay, angels, just get to bed by ten. And be sure to help Franny clean up. And

Allie, I know you're excited about the understudy thing, but don't stay on the phone all night. And Mattie, no TV, and stay off the Internet—"

"Good night, Mom. Have a good time," they chorused.

"Alone at last." Ted grinned, grabbing my hand as the door closed behind us.

I stopped at the bottom of the steps. "Where's the uniform?"

"Don't you trust me? Plainclothes guy in the blue Olds near the corner." He nodded at a car parked two houses down from mine.

"Can he watch the house from that far away?"

"Believe me, nothing gets by this guy. Between him and the alarm system, your little ones are safer than if you were guarding them yourself."

"They're not so little anymore," I murmured mournfully as I slid into the deep bucket seat of his Miata and buckled my belt. "Allie's in love."

"Ah, so. And who's the lucky guy?"

"Her leading man. Well, *the* leading man. She got to rehearse with him today because the girl playing Yum-Yum didn't show. He's really cute. But he's seventeen, too old for her."

"So it's a crush. Let her enjoy it."

"So long as it stays that way."

"Man, you are one tough mama."

"Being a parent *is* tough," I declared passionately, "and believe me, being essentially a single parent who works is—"

"So I've heard about two hundred times. Tell me, what'd you think of the new patient I sent you?"

"I liked him. He invited us to dinner, by the way. He's a real charmer."

"You think so?"

"Me and the rest of the American public. Don't you?"

'He has charisma."

"And I'm a miracle-worker. He said to tell you you're very lucky."

Ted pulled me close. "I knew that."

"So long as you still think so after dinner," I murmured, resting my head against his shoulder.

He removed his arm and my head. "Uh-oh," he said.

I managed to stall him till he'd finished his second glass of wine. He'd let me get away with the stall because he was tired and hungry and not eager to get into an argument, but his expression turned grim when I described the attempted kidnapping. "Why didn't you tell me about this before?"

"I did call you, Ted. As soon as Meg and I found a phone, we—"

"But what were you doing there in the first place?"

"I needed some Rescue Remedy."

"You needed what?"

"Rescue Remedy for my pain and stress. You can only get it in a health-food store."

"And they only carry it in this one store where Laurel just happened to work."

"Well, actually, I got it in another place, but Meg wanted some—"

"Spare me. You went to find Laurel."

"All right. But it was only because I'd messed you up before and I wanted to make amends. Which I did, because I found her." I picked up the menu and studied it. "The rack of lamb looks good. What do you feel like?"

"Would it surprise you to learn your little bird and her charge had flown the coop by the time my men got there?"

"Well, we couldn't tie her up."

"So d'you think maybe it might've been better if you'd left well enough alone and let us find her?"

"Those kidnappers would've gotten that girl if we hadn't been there," I protested. "She's illegal, Ted. She was so frightened and begged us not to call the police. I'd hate to be responsible for her being picked up by Immigration."

He put down his glass and looked me in the eye. "You'd rather see her kidnapped and forced into prostitution."

"No, of course not, but—"

Our waitress appeared at Ted's elbow, smiling, pencil poised. "Have you decided what you want yet?"

I was too upset to make such an important decision. "Uh—could you give us a minute?"

The smile disappeared. "No problem."

When she'd gone, Ted covered my hand with his. "Carrie, the people involved in this sex-trade business are the worst kind of murderous thugs. They're outlaws even among the outlaws."

"I know. I have a patient who told me. I just think there has to be an alternative for this girl between going back to abject poverty or being a sex slave."

"If Laurel can get the girl to testify, we can close The Land of Oz down. It'll put a crimp in the trade and save a few others from a similar fate."

I stared at the picture on the wall, peaceful blue and

green water lilies, thinking how life was such a game of chance. Where one was born and under what circumstances determined so much. "Laurel's not going to turn herself in so long as she thinks you think she's the murderer."

"Do you think she is?"

"I did for a while but, I don't know, it's just too pat." He surprised me. "I agree."

"Really?"

"She's not the only suspect."

"Who else?" I asked eagerly.

"Uh-uh. No more questions. What do you want to eat?"

I glanced at the menu. "I'll have the pasta special. Maybe Laurel's right. Maybe Helena stiffed the yakuza, or maybe a relative of—no, it doesn't explain Grasso or Klinger. Those are the puzzle pieces that don't fit."

He smiled. "You want an appetizer?"

"No. You suppose Jenny or her parents know where she is?"

"It's a good bet." He was quiet for a minute. I watched as he carefully broke off a piece of bread and buttered it. "You think you can get them to tell you?"

"I might, if I could assure them she won't be held."

"I don't have enough evidence to hold her. Tell them to have her come in with a lawyer. I just want to talk to her."

"There's one other thing I think I could help with."

"Don't push it."

I leaned forward in my chair. "Would you let me talk to Andrew?"

"He says he can't remember anything."

"I was with him when he got hit. He started to tell me

something. I might be able to jog his memory. Or maybe I could try a little alpha-theta training. You remember how that worked with Meg in Key West."

"Meg was a willing subject."

"Well, I'm persuasive."

"I'll say."

"Will you do it?"

He leaned back in his chair and swirled the wine in his glass, peering at me with half-closed eyes over the rim. "I must be either drunk or crazy, but okay, I'll set it up. Only, though, if you promise me this is the end of the line for you. No more going off on your own."

"Deal." I clicked his glass with mine.

"When this is over, you want to take a week off and go skiing?"

My heart fluttered. I hadn't been on a vacation in so long, I'd forgotten that people actually do go away and have fun. I suppressed my initial reaction, which was to say, *"I can't. What'll I do about the children?"* Because they'd gone skiing with their father last Christmas and maybe I could take a few days off before the holidays this year and they could stay with him. Things were always slow in my office before Christmas. Maybe it was finally my turn.

I smiled broadly, even though it hurt my split lip. "Ouch," I said. "I'd love to."

"No ifs, ands, or buts? I'm amazed."

"Well, if we can just get this killer locked up by the end of the month—"

"If *who* can get him locked up?"

"Oops. You, you, I meant you."

11

✦

I ARRIVED AT THE HOSPITAL a little after five o'clock the next evening. The cop outside Andrew's door had obviously been told to let me pass and did so without comment after he'd checked my picture ID.

Andrew was sitting up in an armchair, listlessly picking at a dinner that looked like something Horty would refuse—and Horty has no problem rooting through garbage cans. The bandage the doctors had wound around his head actually made him appear sexy, adding a sort of rakish, piratelike air to his striking good looks. People like that don't turn black and blue like the rest of us mortals. In Andrew's case the bruises only emphasized the indigo color of his eyes, and where my skin had turned a jaundiced yellow, his just looked attractively smudged.

"Hello, Andrew."

He gave a little jump, clearly startled at having his

solitude disturbed. "I'm not supposed to have visitors," he exclaimed nervously. "Who let you in here?"

I moved closer so he could get a good look at my war wounds. "Don't you remember me? I'm Laurel Herman's friend. I was talking to you outside the school when the —when someone threw whatever it was broke your car window. You fell on me."

I thought I saw a flash of recognition in his eyes, but he looked away and mumbled, "I don't remember talking to you."

I pretended I hadn't heard. "You were telling me I should advise Laurel to turn herself in, that she should tell the police about her mother—or the money—or something. . . ." I paused, waiting for him to select from column A, B, or C.

He began pushing something green and slimy that bore a minimal resemblance to some vegetable around on his plate. "I told you. It's all a blur. I don't remember anything about what happened on Friday."

"Don't worry," I said cheerfully, hoisting my rear end onto the foot of the bed. "I couldn't remember at first either. It'll come back."

He shoved the tray aside and stood up. "I've had a concussion, and I'm still a little dizzy. I need to lie down."

"Go ahead," I said obligingly, sliding back off the bed. "I'll sit in the chair."

Not bothering to remove his silk robe, he crawled under the sheet. "I don't understand why that cop let you in. They're supposed to be protecting me."

"I'm hardly a danger to you," I said. "I've been thinking that whoever threw that thing might've been aiming for me."

"You think so?" The self-centered creep sat up, suddenly hopeful, as though if it were only me they were after, everything would be just hunky-dory. "Why? Why would someone want to hurt you?"

I had him hooked, so I played along. "I'm Laurel's friend. I've been trying to help her, and whoever's been setting her up wouldn't want—"

He glanced at me sharply. "What do you mean, setting her up?"

"Don't you think she's being set up? The way I figure it, someone wants it to look like Laurel killed Helena Forester and meant to kill you and Donald Grasso. It didn't come out in the papers till Sunday about the will, so when you and I were attacked, Laurel didn't know about the provision that she wouldn't inherit unless— well, unless you were out of the picture."

"I didn't know about the will before it was read," he said. "Helena never discussed money with me."

This guy's memory seemed just fine to me. "Did you know she was sick?"

"She'd lost a lot of weight, but she told me she was dieting."

How could you be married to someone, I wondered, *and not know they were fatally ill?*

"Helena was a very stoic woman," he said defensively, as though I'd said the words. "She would never have admitted she was that sick."

"Not even to you?"

"Not even to herself, damn her."

And damned she probably is. "Why do you think she set the will up the way she did?"

He shifted around in the bed, straightened the sheet, finally kicked it off. "She was—Helena didn't forgive easily. If she liked you she could be very generous, but if she didn't, God help you. She and Laurel—well, I guess you know Laurel blamed her for her mother's death. I guess the will was Helena's way of punishing her."

"Why bother? The will didn't change Laurel's situation. All it did was put you and Grasso in jeopardy. Would Helena have wanted to hurt either of you for any reason?"

"No, no. I can't think of any reason. Helena and I were getting along fine," he responded too quickly.

"She was the jealous type, I hear. That time you danced with Jenny Margolies at the charity ball . . . Did she have any reason to suspect that you and Jenny—"

"No, God, no. I wouldn't be stupid enough to do that."

Still, it must be great not to have to worry anymore, I thought. *To be free and with megabucks.*

"You think the will was the reason she wanted to meet with Laurel? To flaunt it in her face?"

He hesitated before answering. "I hope not."

"Why do you say that?"

"Because it would mean Laurel might have known about the stipulations of the will before the rest of us did."

Which was exactly what I'd been thinking myself on Saturday, so why did it annoy me to hear it coming out of his mouth now?

I rose and walked over to the bed. "Do you believe Laurel killed your wife?"

"I—don't know what to believe. I know it looked bad for me when Helena was killed, but I wouldn't've benefited from Grasso's death, and Laurel's the only one who benefits if something happens to me. I just wish she'd turn herself in."

And maybe it was just that simple, but I couldn't resist baiting him. "Well, if she does and someone tries to kill you again, we'll know it isn't Laurel."

He scowled, obviously failing to grasp the humor of that, so I changed the subject. "Tell me about Helena's travel agency."

His face closed up like someone had pulled down a shade. "I'm a math teacher. That's my profession. Other than taking a few trips with my wife, I wasn't involved in her business at all."

"I'll bet you got to stay in all the four-star hotels in Tokyo and Hong Kong, though," I commented. "I hear some of them come complete with your own personal hot and cold running geishas."

Wrong.

His eyes frosted over. "I wish you'd leave. I'm in mourning, and that was a really tasteless remark." -

I wanted to bite my tongue. It wasn't that I believed he was grieving, but my remark had been tactless to say the least and I hadn't wanted to turn him off. "I'm sorry," I said.

"Please go," he replied and turned his back on me.

There was nothing I could do but comply. How was I going to explain to Ted that the subject of putting him into an alpha state hadn't even come up?

On Wednesday morning, at Ted's insistence, I went to his office in Hackensack. He showed me the throwing star that had been aimed at Andrew's and my heads. I'd also seen the mean-looking nunchaku that had just missed Donald Grasso.

"You don't want to get mixed up with these boys," Ted said. "They don't fool around. You understand that?"

"I'm not stupid." I have to admit, looking at the spiky metal star still caked with dried blood (whether Andrew's or mine I didn't ask) was a sobering experience. "Can anybody buy weapons like these?"

"Easily. Through martial-arts magazines."

"So if someone wanted the murder to look like a yakuza gang killing—"

"Sure. But these people are for hire and they're good at what they do, so as far as you're concerned, you can assume—"

"Okay, you've made your point. I'll try to talk to Jenny's parents tonight and then I'm out of it."

I waved to Dan as I passed his desk on my way out, got in my car, and went shopping at Riverside Mall. I felt an overwhelming urge to treat myself to something totally frivolous. At Bath & Body Works I bought a jar of "replenishing botanical bath soak" and some "relaxing bath bubbles with skin-soothing chamomile." I figured I could use all the replenishing I could get, and if chamomile was good for what ailed me internally, it'd be good for what ailed me externally. After that I went to the Gap and ran up my AmEx bill shopping for the kids. It is virtually impossible for me to treat myself without including Allie and Matt. I'm not saying that's a healthy attitude; it's a hang-up having to do with divorce guilt, which is why kids from broken homes tend to have cluttered rooms and screwed-up values. My children are lucky, since my credit-card limits have saved them from such a fate.

I called Jenny's parents' home and got their machine, decided not to leave a message. Better to catch them off guard this evening. I spent the rest of my day off doing errands and mulling over my conversation with Andrew Klinger. That he was an extremely egocentric, materialistic guy was no surprise. That he was nervous and afraid was understandable. That he seemingly, with great reluctance, had managed to implicate Laurel was food for thought. And more food for thought, I realized, was that, without even mentioning her name, Donald Grasso had done the same thing.

Which got me to thinking about the will again. If Laurel was being framed, somebody was doing a real neat job. Who would benefit if Laurel went to jail? Klinger and Grasso's inheritance wouldn't change. They'd get their interest on Helena's money whether Laurel went to jail or not. Besides which, someone had attacked both of them, and my poor head was witness to the fact that the attackers weren't kidding around. The only person who stood to benefit would be the killer, because if Laurel were indicted, the case would be closed.

Unless Helena's will had been forged! There was a thought. If Laurel was right and Grasso had forged Laurel's father's will, what was to stop him from forging Helena's will? That was easy. He was a rich man today, a celebrity. But as Laurel had concluded, unless he was insane no amount of money would be worth his jeopardizing what he'd worked for all his life. As surviving spouse, Klinger would have gotten a third of the estate no matter what the will said, so he had no reason to risk everything by forging a will. Which left who? Or better yet—what? The Foundation. If Klinger, Grasso, and

Laurel were all out of the picture, would the money go to the Foundation? Ten to one it would. The more I thought about it, the more convinced I became that this avenue had to be explored. I was pretty certain Laurel, as a contingent beneficiary, had a right to contest the will. If she did that, she could get an expert—one of those forensics document people—to examine it and determine if it were valid. Why hadn't she done that with her mother's will, I wondered?

I glanced at my watch as I came out of the Pathmark on New Bridge Road. Four-ten. Loading my ten bags of groceries into the trunk, I headed for Piermont, running over my schedule in my head. Franny was expecting me at five. Because Ted was still adamant about her not sleeping alone in her apartment, we'd decided she'd stay open till it began to get dark, at which time I'd pick her up and take her home with me. Matt was getting picked up from soccer practice by the car pool, so I had to get him at Jeff's. I'd get Allie at rehearsal by five-thirty, have the groceries unpacked, animals walked and fed by six, dinner on the table by six-thirty, finished by seven-thirty, make it to the Margolies's by eight. It would mean leaving Franny alone with the kids, but with the alarm now in place, I was fairly comfortable going out for a short time.

Franny was waiting, coat on, just inside her door. She locked up and slid into the passenger seat next to me.

"You're prompt," she said.

"Tight schedule," I replied. "How was your day?"

"Fine. Mr. Yoshida came in."

"No kidding."

"We chatted for a while and he bought an old abacus."

"A what?"

209

"An abacus. It's a frame with beads. The Japanese used to use them to count with."

"I thought they were from China."

"No. Originally Japan."

I shut up. I've learned when and with whom not to argue.

Allie was bouncing up and down impatiently as I pulled up. One glance at her face and I knew Sophie hadn't shown up. I turned to look at her as she jumped into the backseat.

"Guess what?" she sang.

"I know. I'm happy for you, sweetie. What's the story with Sophie?"

"Nobody knows. She just hasn't called and doesn't show. Mr. Creighton is disgusted with her, so I get to be Yum-Yum." She failed miserably at keeping the excitement off her face. "It's not my fault, though. I really didn't wish bad on her."

"Of course you didn't. And you'll be wonderful in the part. Just make sure it doesn't affect your schoolwork," I added like a dutiful mother as I pulled into the driveway.

By seven forty-five I was on my way to the Margolies's. I hadn't called again. I couldn't have even if I'd wanted to. As soon as dinner was over, Allie was on the phone spreading the news to her friends and her father. At precisely 8:05 I was standing on the doorstep of the Margolies's stone and half-timber home on Park Street. I think Park Street is one of the prettiest streets in Tenafly. The landscaping around the houses has been in for fifty or sixty years, and the foliage has a beauty that comes only with age. *Too bad it doesn't work that way with people,* I thought as I rang the doorbell.

"Who is it?" a voice called out.

"It's Carrie Carlin, Mrs. Margolies." There was no response, and I realized there was a remote possibility Jenny's mother didn't recognize my name. "Jenny's a patient of mine. May I talk to you, please?"

The door opened and I came face to face with Jenny twenty-five years from now, right down to the green eyes and the splash of freckles across the nose.

"Jenny's not here," said her clone.

"You must've heard this a million times," I said, "but the resemblance is amazing."

"Yes, I know. What can I do for you, Ms. Carlin?"

There was a distinct chill in her voice. Clearly, I could forget about being warmly taken into the bosom of the family.

"Is Mr. Margolies at home? I'd like to talk to both of you."

She hesitated, then said, "Come in."

I followed her through a terra-cotta-tiled foyer to the living room of my dreams. A fire was burning low in a fireplace framed by a carved wood mantelpiece on which stood a large bronze sculpture. The floor was covered with a thick gray-green carpet, and the walls were hung with paintings from the French impressionist school, which is my favorite. Mr. Margolies, a slightly built man with a short graying beard and mustache, was seated in front of a huge picture window that overlooked a garden and a swimming pool in the backyard. He rose when his wife and I entered the room. I shook his hand as she introduced us and took a seat in one of the glove-leather chairs that formed a friendly conversation area around the fireplace.

"What a beautiful room," I said.

"Thank you," responded Mr. M.

Mrs. M. said nothing.

"Look, I'll get right to the point," I began uncomfortably. "I know you and Jenny care about Laurel, and I'm sure you want to do the right thing for her. But if—"

"Ms. Carlin," Mr. Margolies interrupted. "Laurel has had nothing but grief in her life since her father got involved with Helena Forester. But if you and your policeman friend think she was capable of—"

"I don't believe she killed Helena Forester. I did at one point, but I've had second thoughts. And Lieutenant Brodsky only wants to talk to her." I proceeded to tell them about my theory that the will was a forgery and that someone at the Foundation was probably behind it. "That's where the money will probably go if all the named beneficiaries are eliminated," I explained. "Laurel can contest the will. She has the right to have it examined. If I'm right it will lead us to the murderer, Laurel will be off the hook, and she'll be able to work with the police in helping stop the practice of using girls like—"

"Like Sophida," said a voice I was coming to know quite well.

And so I learned that little Sophie Maitini of Yum-Yum fame was the girl Meg and I had helped rescue from a fate truly worse than death.

"Where is she now?" I asked Laurel.

"With Jenny. Safe, for the moment."

"But she's illegal, isn't she? You said—"

"When this gets straightened out I'll find a way to sponsor her. She'll work for me at Jasmania."

I rose. "You all agree Laurel should come with me to talk to Lieutenant Brodsky? He's assured me that's all he wants to do at the moment."

A look passed between the couple. Laurel shrugged and nodded. Mr. Margolies reached for the phone. "Tomorrow," he said. "I'll call my lawyer."

I looked at Laurel. "How do I know you won't disappear again?"

"You'll just have to take my word for it," she replied. "The same way I'm taking yours that your detective friend won't lock me up."

After a pause I said, "I'll pick you up at eleven-thirty."

I was driving home when I thought about Marlene Beasley and the Foundation and how I'd like to know who was on the board. It was late to drop in on someone you hardly know—past nine o'clock—but I was in Tenafly, which is only a hop, skip, and a jump from Englewood, so I decided to chance it.

Marlene answered the door in her robe and slippers after peeking through a peephole and unlocking three dead bolts. I apologized profusely for stopping by so late. "I just need a list of the people on the board," I said.

She stared at me blankly.

"For the article," I explained. I'd like to mention who's on the board of the Foundation."

"Oh. Oh, dear. I'll have to get it out of my files. I'll send it to you."

"Don't you know who they are?" I asked.

"Well," she said, annoyance seeping through her normally courteous manner. "It is late. Do you have to know this minute?"

"I'm sorry," I lied, "I have a deadline for the article."

She sighed and tapped her foot impatiently. "Well, let's see. Helena, of course, was the president. My husband, Ben, is acting president now. Janet Sexton is secretary, and Donald Grasso's our treasurer. We voted Andrew on the board last year to fill Dorene Hillerman's spot when she moved to California. Helena insisted on that. This year Tomo Yoshida came on when Brian Pendleton became ill. Then there's me and Katherine Carpenter—"

"Excuse me," I said, stunned. "Did you say Yoshida? Tomo Yoshida?"

"Yes. A lovely Japanese gentleman. An associate of Helena's. Came on just a few weeks before she—before she passed on."

Maybe Yoshida is a name like Smith, I told myself as I drove down East Clinton Avenue at a speed that would've definitely gotten me a ticket if I'd been spotted by the local gendarmes. *Maybe Tomo Yoshida is like Tom Smith, so there could be as many Tomo Yoshidas in Japan as there are Tom Smiths here.*

Yeah, and maybe God's in his heaven and all's right with the world. Only I didn't know where God was at the moment and all wasn't right in my world. Mr. Yoshida, who had appeared in my office just a week before, shortly after Helena Forester's murder, was on the board of Helena's foundation, and Mr. Yoshida had been oddly wary of having me monitor his responses, as though afraid I could read his mind, and Mr. Yoshida had known about the Gurentai yakuza, and, I thought with a sinking feeling in the pit of my stomach, Mr. Yoshida had been displaying an inordinate amount of interest in Franny Gold's antiques.

It was after ten o'clock by the time I pulled into the driveway. The kids and Franny were asleep. Horty greeted me at the door and, sensing my distress the way dogs do, licked my hand and stayed close to me, getting under my feet as I wandered around checking on the kids and turning off lights. José looked up from the foot of Matt's bed and trilled a greeting. Lucie rolled over and purred, inviting me to scratch his belly, which I did and immediately felt calmer. I once told Ted that in my next life I'm coming back as one of my own cats, and he told me I'd better make sure I'd be guaranteed nine lives because being around me for any length of time wasn't safe for any living creature.

I called Ted right after that, but he wasn't home and he wasn't at the precinct. The sergeant on the desk told me he'd been called out on a murder case, which always puts the kibosh on my night's sleep. I left a message saying it was urgent I speak with him and I would be in his office at noon tomorrow accompanied by Laurel Herman and her lawyer.

I didn't want to wake Franny and tell her about Mr. Yoshida, so there was nothing else I could do until the morning.

I got undressed, took my pillow and a blanket, and, followed by my canine shadow, went downstairs to the couch and mindlessly watched some repeat TV sitcoms till my eyes closed. Eventually I fell off.

In my dreams Mr. Yoshida is sitting in the recliner in my office, all hooked up to the computer. I'm watching the monitor as his EDR goes off the screen. No matter how many times I adjust the numbers, his stress level keeps going higher and higher. I take a pack of stress cards from a shelf, handing him one after the other, and on one after the other, the patch turns black and he tosses them aside.

I came wide awake and sat bolt upright in bed, or to be literal, on the couch. Mr. Yoshida had never been hooked up to the computer's EDR measurement, but he had used my biofeedback stress cards. I had Mr. Yoshida's thumbprint as clear as day on a stress card in his patient folder in my office.

12

✦

By ELEVEN-THIRTY the next morning I was on my way to the Margolies's to pick up Laurel. I'd debated telling Allie about Sophie but decided to put it off. I have a pretty open relationship with my daughter. We've had frank discussions about sex but I was going to have to give some real thought to how I would explain Sophie's situation.

I was able to reschedule my morning patients, so I was free until my ADDS started coming after school. I planned to go by the office to pick up Tomo Yoshida's stress card, and I told Franny I'd drop her off at her shop then. We left the house, and drove to Tenafly first, even though it meant I'd have to backtrack to Piermont. I didn't want to be late for Laurel, afraid she'd disappear on me again. On the way I brought Franny up to date about Yoshida.

"Mr. Yoshida," she kept saying. "I can't believe it. He seemed such a nice man."

"So did Ted Bundy," I replied, sounding to my own ears like Ted Brodsky. "Think about it, Franny. It all ties in. He was probably Helena's liaison with the people in Japan who set up the tours."

"Maybe, but he didn't kill her."

"We don't know that."

"He wasn't the one riding the bike that day."

I shot her a quick glance. "What're you talking about? You didn't see the person."

"But I got an impression. The bike rider was big. His hands with that tattoo were big. Mr. Yoshida is a relatively small man."

I shrugged. "So it was one of those hired yakuza thugs. It makes no difference if he did the actual killing. He's involved in that whole sex-tour thing. He has to be. It's all too coincidental."

"But the killer wasn't Japanese."

I slammed on the brakes. "What did you say?"

"I said the killer wasn't Japanese. He was Caucasian."

"How do you know that? You said you didn't see him up close."

"I know, but I saw his hands. And his hair, he was wearing a hat, but what I saw of his hair—well, it wasn't dark."

"Did you tell the police that?" A car honked impatiently and I hit the accelerator.

"I think I must have. I was so nervous I don't remember quite what I said. Wouldn't they have asked me?"

"I'm sure they did."

"I'm usually very observant. I can look at someone and

almost always tell their ethnicity. Like I knew Walawon was Thai."

I could see she was getting upset, so I forbore mentioning that what she'd known was that Walawon was a Thai name. And the first time she'd seen Laurel in her shop she hadn't noticed that she was part Asian.

"No one could blame you if you didn't get it right that day," I said soothingly and stopped questioning her. We stayed pretty silent the rest of the way to Tenafly.

Laurel came out of the Margolies's house as soon as I beeped the horn. I breathed a sigh of relief as she opened the back door and got into the car.

"Mr. Margolies's lawyer will meet us at Lieutenant Brodsky's office," she said.

"Fine," I replied as I pulled away from the curb. "You remember Franny, don't you? I have to drop her off in Piermont and pick up something in my office, and then we'll be on our way."

Laurel nodded and murmured a hello.

When I got to the corner and was making the turn onto East Clinton Avenue, I began repeating the conversation Franny and I had just had about Mr. Yoshida and the killer on the bike. When Laurel didn't respond, I stopped at the red light at the intersection and glanced over my shoulder. "Laurel, did you hear me? Franny says the—"

"Run the light," Laurel hissed. "We're being followed."

I glanced into my rearview mirror and saw a green Lexus behind us. "What makes you think—" I started to ask, when the black car behind the Lexus suddenly pulled around it, trying to nose in.

Dinosaur! Tyrannosaurus rex! This is a life-threatening situation, screamed my internal fight-or-flight response, and my adrenaline started pumping. I took off right through the red. I once got a seventy-dollar ticket, which cost me an additional two hundred dollars a year on my insurance for the next three years, for doing forty-five on Engle Street. The cops love to hide out on the little side streets. Not this morning, though. I was doing sixty, honking and screeching through stop signs. No cops. And all the time my heart was racing, my mind was keeping pace. Who would be chasing us? Out of the corner of my eye, I caught a glimpse of Franny, who had gone pale and rigid. Did the killer still believe Franny knew something? Well, maybe she did. She'd just remembered he was Caucasian, hadn't she? Maybe I should try doing alpha-theta with her. Maybe she'd come up with a description. Or was it Laurel they were after? What had she learned about the sex-tour business that might bring down other people besides Helena Forester? Maybe it was me they wanted to get. Me and my insufferable curiosity that was always landing me in shit.

Fortunately, I know the area pretty well and I'd had a jump on the sedan. I made a quick left onto Hudson, another onto Prospect, a right, another right, and I was on County Road, zooming toward Cresskill doing fifty in a twenty-five-mile zone. Still no cops. And no black sedan. "I think we lost them," I shouted. "Laurel, do you see—"

Suddenly, there it was flying out of a side street and coming almost even with us. There was a blue sports vehicle in front of me. No way I could see over it or pass it. The window of the sedan went down, and I saw a gun poke out. Not a short, snubbed-nosed thing either. Something with a long barrel like you see in Dirty Harry movies. "Get down," I yelled. Reaching over, I somehow managed to release Franny's seat belt and push her onto the floor. She gave a little yelp of pain. *Oh, God,* I thought, *I've broken her hip! Well,* an inner voice responded crazily, *a hip break's better than a hole in the head.*

I assumed Laurel was taking care of herself as I began zigzagging and honking the horn. I thought I heard the crack of a rifle shot, but I wasn't sure. The guy in the car in front of me suddenly seemed to wake up to what was happening, and veered off into a driveway. I accelerated right through another red, heard sirens as I cut left onto Madison. Our pursuer made a fast right. I was all over the road as the Honda shimmied and I shook. It took me a block to bring us both under control. I pulled into King's parking lot, brought the car to a stop, and lay my head down on the steering wheel, dry-mouthed and panting like a dog who'd been locked up all day in a hot van. Franny was trying to crawl back onto the seat, and I stretched out an arm and tugged at her sleeve, trying to help. The sirens got louder, and two police cars roared right past us down Union Street. When I could catch my breath, I raised my head. "Everyone okay?" I whispered.

"Y-yes," Franny answered in a small voice.

Thank God, no broken hip. I turned around. Laurel's eyes were closed and she was leaning back against the seat. My first thought was that she'd been hit, but I couldn't see any blood. "Laurel?" I cried. She opened her eyes.

"I'm okay," she said. "Just a little shaken up, and kicking myself that I left my gun at the Margolies's." She gave me a small grin. "Nice driving, Carrie. Right up there with Mario Andretti."

"Thanks a bunch." With clammy hands I managed to turn the key and start the engine. I didn't want to hang around. Who knew if those guys would be back? "Okay, let's think this through," I said, trying my best to stop shaking so I could assess the situation rationally. "Somebody's pretty obviously trying to kill one of us. Which means the killer is afraid one of us knows something that could identify him. So which one of us knows something we don't know we know?"

No takers.

"Franny, you're starting to remember things you saw the day of Helena's murder, which could lead to the killer. But the killer doesn't know that, so Laurel, you're the most likely candidate."

"It probably is me they're after," she said quietly. "I have proof that The Land of Oz sets up sex tours in Japan. They bring girls illegally into this country and use them against their will to service their clients. We're talking huge money. So while Helena was primarily responsible for the travel agency's involvement, there have to be others who might like to see me disappear."

"Who?" I asked. "The yakuza? Is the Foundation involved? Is Yoshida the liaison?"

"Maybe all of the above—I don't know yet, but the people I work with are pretty certain Helena Forester was only the tip of a very ugly iceberg."

The puzzle pieces were beginning to fall into place.

I slowed at a light and turned to look at Laurel. "I'm curious about something else," I said. "What really happened that day in Franny's shop between you and Helena? What you said about arguing over the price of a necklace was a lie, wasn't it?"

Laurel fingered the jade pendant she was wearing around her neck. "Not totally. This was my mother's. My father gave it to her on their honeymoon. It's a unique piece, one of a kind—very valuable. For me it has sentimental value, but Helena always wanted it. I never let her get her greedy hands on it. When I was a kid I used to sleep with it on."

"But why'd she want to see you? Why'd she ask you to meet her?"

"I never found out. My own fault—she started to say if I'd give her the pendant, she'd tell me something I'd always wanted to know, and before I heard her out I threw in her face the information I had on the illegals and the sex tours. I told her I didn't have to make a deal with the devil because I had information that was going to send her straight to hell where she belonged. I didn't, of course," she added wryly, "mean it literally."

"I heard you say something about time being short," Franny said.

"I told her her time was running out, but I wasn't implying it was because I planned to kill her," Laurel replied. "She laughed in my face because she knew her time really was running out and she was going to escape me. The last thing I ever wanted was to see her dead. I wanted her to suffer. If she'd lived she'd have gone to jail and my parents could have rested in peace."

"Why didn't you contest your father's will?"

Laurel's laugh was bitter. "You have any idea what that kind of thing costs? Forget that no lawyer would've taken the case of a seventeen-year-old with no money. I spoke to one who told me straight out, Helena had the money, she had the power."

I'd learned about money and power during my divorce.

"She'd hire a high-priced law firm who'd paper me to death. If my expert said the will was phony, she'd get five to say it wasn't. I wouldn't win and I'd end up in debt."

I couldn't think of a thing to say after that. Neither could Franny. We rode in silence until I pulled up in front of Meg's Place.

"I don't think you should open your shop today, Franny," I said. "Yoshida might come in when you're there all alone. Tell Meg what's going on and stay here with her till I get back from Ted's."

She didn't give me an argument. There's nothing like a good old-fashioned car chase to give someone religion. She got out and went into the café. I pulled ahead, made a left into my driveway, and parked in the lot behind my building.

"I need to get a stress card out of my files," I told Laurel. "You want to come up with me?"

"Strength in numbers," she replied, opening the car door. "I just wish I had my gun."

"I have a sword," I said, grinning, and opened up the trunk. I drew out the samurai sword, unsheathed it, and held it up. The shiny blade gleamed wickedly in the sunlight.

"Where'd you get that?"

"It's Franny's—a prop for *The Mikado*. The powers that be don't want it kept at the school. For obvious reasons that I should've realized. I was going to take it home, but, what the hell, I'll keep it here in the office. One never knows when a samurai sword'll come in handy." I said it jokingly, but I kept the sword unsheathed as we made our way into the building and rode the elevator to the third floor.

Tomo Yoshida, carrying a very large shopping bag,

was loitering in the hallway outside my office. I literally broke out in a cold sweat at the sight of him.

"Mr. Yoshida," I exclaimed, forcing a smile and trying to keep my voice steady. "What're you doing here? You don't have an appointment today."

"Ah, yes, you're correct, but I brought you the sandals and the fans I promised you. For the play," he added, as I stood dumbly staring at him.

"Oh. Oh, yes, thank you. Thank you very much. I'll take them. Um—"

"Are you all right? You seem upset."

"No. I mean, yes, I'm fine."

"Well, your hands seem to be full," he said, eyeing the sword. "I'll put them in your office for you. Do you have your keys?"

"Give me the sword," Laurel whispered, taking it out of my hands. I began searching in my purse for the keys, heard my phone ringing as I found them, but I was having trouble inserting the key into the lock. By the time I pushed the door open, the ringing had stopped. I held out my hands for the bag. "Thanks again, Mr. Yoshida," I babbled. "I'm sure Mr. Creighton and everyone—my daughter, everyone in the cast—uh—they'll be very appreciative—um—how much do we owe—"

He walked past me into the reception area and deposited the bag onto one of the chairs.

"Nothing. No charge. My pleasure. I bought the sandals in small, medium, and large, so there should be something for everyone. When is the first performance?"

"Two weeks from next Saturday. I—I'll send you tickets. Um—well, thanks again. . . . "

There was a lengthy, very awkward pause as we stood smiling inanely at each other. Laurel remained by the door, unsheathed sword in hand. Mr. Yoshida bowed politely, started out, then stopped in the doorway. "I see you have the sword back," he said to me. "Is it possible they're not using it in the operetta and it's now for sale?"

"Oh, no," I said quickly. "They're using it. I'm just holding it for the time being."

"Well," he said pleasantly, "remind Ms. Gold that I have—ah, what is it you Americans say?—first dibs on it." And he left.

You can have the finger, I have dibs on the thumb flashed wildly, crazily through my mind as I headed for the little anteroom off my office where I keep my file cabinet. I riffled through my client folders, pulled Yoshida's stress card, carefully wrapped it in a piece of paper, and stuffed it into my purse. As I went back into my office I decided to take a few minutes and run through Yoshida's last session tape. I noticed that my message light was blinking, but I was anxious to see if he'd let anything slip that might be significant, so I ignored it and flipped the tape into the recorder.

"I need a few more minutes, Laurel," I called out. "Just want to listen to a section of last Monday's sessions."

I rewound to the beginning of Yoshida's session, then fast-forwarded to the end, skipping the part where I was doing all the talking. Nothing incriminating that I could catch, but I decided to bring the tape with me to the precinct. Ted's instincts were better honed than mine. Grasso's session followed Yoshida's, and I found myself listening, mesmerized by that sonorous voice. Halfway through, I ejected the tape and dropped it into my purse. Then I pressed the message button on my answering machine.

Ted's voice. *"Carrie, if you're there, stay there. Keep Laurel and Franny with you in your office. Lock the door, and don't let anybody in but me. I'm on my way."*

What was that all about? Why was Ted coming here instead of waiting for us? What had happened that he wanted us to lock ourselves in? I reached for the phone, thinking I might catch him before he left. "Laurel?" I called as I started to dial. "Lock the door. There's a message on my machine from Ted. He wants us to—"

She wasn't answering me, and I realized she hadn't answered me earlier. My hand froze. "Laurel? You out there?"

Oh, God, I thought. *She's run again. Ted'll have me drawn and quartered.*

I dropped the phone and dashed out to the waiting room. The door leading to the hallway was wide open, and Laurel was nowhere to be seen. Scattered all over the floor were one-toed socks, sandals, and half-open fans, as though someone had grabbed the shopping bag and thrown it so that it hit the wall with enough force to tear it open.

"Laurel!" I shouted as the realization dawned that Laurel hadn't left of her own free will.

"Laurel, Laurel." The echo reverberated off the walls of the empty room. I started for the hallway, tripped over what I thought was a sandal, and fell to my knees, gasping as I realized I'd just missed slicing my calf open with the blade of the sword. I grabbed the handle, was starting to get to my feet when I saw that something had been scratched into the floor. For one heart-stopping minute I thought it was a star. But it wasn't. It was a letter. The letter Y. Laurel had managed to keep her hands on the sword long enough to let me know who her kidnapper was! Yoshida. Then I looked again. The Y

was scrawled in cursive and the loop ended abruptly, as though the sword had been dropped quickly, but the top of the letter seemed to be rounded and almost closed. Which could make it a different letter. Which could make it a G.

Clutching the sword in one hand and my car keys in the other, I took the steps two at a time and was out of the building in seconds, my eyes frantically sweeping the street for some sign of Laurel, praying I'd hear sirens, knowing it was too soon for Ted to get here. I dashed across the street to the liquor store and asked a man just about to enter if he'd seen a young woman with long dark hair walking with a Japanese man or maybe she was with an American man or possibly—but probably not— with a woman. He gave me a funny look, said he hadn't seen anyone, and hurried into the store. I started for Meg's Place, then changed my mind and ran back to my building to wait for Ted, my mind spinning like a tape on fast forward. Where had the killer taken Laurel? And who was it? Who was the bad guy? Yoshida? Or, if indeed the letter was a G—Grasso? But it couldn't be Grasso, because he himself had been a victim. He'd been attacked by the killer. So maybe what looked like a G really was a Y. *Wait a minute,* I thought as another idea came to me. Maybe the Y was for yakuza. Or if it was a G, it was for Gurentai yakuza, and Laurel hadn't had time to finish what she'd started to write. That would make sense. The yakuza had tried to kidnap Sophie and now had kidnapped Laurel. Yoshida must have connections with them, so whether the kidnapper was Yoshida himself or a hired thug, Laurel would be in dire danger.

Franny must have been wrong about the killer being Caucasian. She was getting on, and her eyes weren't as sharp as they once were. On the other hand, they'd been sharp enough to see that tattoo. But the fact remained, Tomo Yoshida had been lurking outside my office on the pretext of bringing me the *Mikado* props this morning, and everything I'd discovered about him yesterday still held true.

I heard the sound of an engine and a familiar-looking black sedan screeched past me heading up toward Nyack. Inside were two occupants: the driver, a man wearing a ski cap, and the passenger, female, small, with long dark hair. Laurel.

"Laurel!" I screamed, but she couldn't hear me. Laurel and—who?

I didn't have time to wait for Ted. Making a snap decision, I flew down the driveway to my car, jumped in, tossed the sword onto the passenger seat, and tore out to the street. There were several vehicles ahead of me on the narrow, two-lane road that leads from the village of Piermont to the tiny village of Grandview-on-the-Hudson. I kept losing sight of the sedan as it rounded the curves, and it was impossible to pass even one car. Desperate to do something to attract attention, I began honking my horn. Drivers coming the other way glared at me, but I kept it up because there was method to my noisiness. If a cop stopped me, he could radio ahead and have the sedan pulled over.

Who was driving that car? His face had gone by so quickly it was a blur, and the ski cap had been pulled low. Next to Laurel he looked to be a large man, but next to Laurel anyone looked large, and you can't really tell size when someone's sitting in a car.

Suddenly something I'd just heard on the tape popped into my mind.

"I guess I'll have to leave that to your friend, the detective, and the antique lady," Donald Grasso had said.

The antique lady. Why would Donald Grasso have mentioned Franny? Franny, the witness. How would he have known that she was the witness unless he'd seen her? It had never been in the papers. The only people who knew that Franny was the witness were the cops, Jenny, Laurel, Meg, Kevin, Ruth-Ann, me—and the killer.

This can't be. I must be missing something, I thought. No one would ever believe that the illustrious Donald Grasso was a kidnapper and a murderer. And he'd been attacked. There was that. No matter how I twisted it around in my head, that puzzle piece just didn't fit. Besides which, he was a celebrity—a respected legal authority, time and again invited to appear on national television. Even Laurel had admitted he had too much to lose, that no amount of money could entice a man of his position to throw it all away. The only blemish—if you could call it that—on his record was his long-term association with Helena Forester, but that was proof he certainly could not be a candidate for her murder. What possible motive could Donald Grasso have had for killing Helena Forester?

My earlier conversation with Laurel began replaying in my mind. Helena had told Laurel she had something to tell her, something that Laurel had always wanted to know. What had she always wanted to know that Helena knew? *The circumstances of her mother's death and her father's will.* Had Grasso really had a hand in those events? If he had, so had Helena. Why would she rat on him when she'd been the beneficiary, and why at this late date? It didn't make sense.

The realization hit with such force it was like being beaned by the throwing star again, only this time, instead of knocking me out, it knocked the cobwebs out. *Because Helena Forester knew she was dying and was therefore untouchable!* At least in this world. But Donald Grasso, her ex-lover, would be ruined.

Why would she have wanted to ruin Donald Grasso? What could have happened between them to turn her against him? Did it have something to do with the sex tours?

I shook my head. I had to stop trying to find answers. I had to concentrate on what I was doing. I was counting on the probability that if the killer had heard me honking and thought I might have seen him, he wouldn't dare to harm Laurel, because to shut me up he'd have to kill me too. Which was an extremely unpleasant thought but remote enough that I was able to push it aside.

The road twisted and turned, and for a moment I lost sight of the sedan. I honked, gunned the engine, attempted to pass the car in front of me, and almost collided head-on with a pickup truck. Why, oh, why hadn't I bought a cell phone? Twenty-five dollars a month, that's why.

An eternity later we came to the outskirts of Nyack, and I caught sight of the sedan as it cut up a side road heading toward the Tappan Zee Bridge. There were now only three cars between us. The killer was driving carefully at the speed limit, apparently, despite the racket I'd been making, unaware that I was tailing him. The traffic was relatively light and moving at a steady pace. I decided to hang back and follow him.

He was about halfway across the bridge, just approaching the overhead steel girders, when it happened. The sedan picked up speed, cut swiftly into the right lane, the passenger door opened, and I saw Laurel hanging half in, half out of the car. The bastard was trying to push her directly out into the path of the traffic!

My brain released about a gallon of adrenaline. Instinctively, I leaned on my horn, gunned the engine, and shot into the middle lane. I didn't know what I planned to do. I only knew I didn't have much time in which to do it. We were neck and neck then, and the driver couldn't miss hearing and seeing me. And I couldn't miss seeing him. The penetrating eyes of Donald Grasso, TV idol, legal eagle, and legend in his own time, looked directly into mine.

I floored the accelerator and pulled in front of him. And slowed. I heard a crack and a tiny spider webbing hole appeared in my windshield just to the right of my head. *Holy shit, the guy really was trying to kill me!* For the first time in my life I thanked God I was short. I slid down as low as I could and still manage to see over the steering wheel. Grasso tried to cut past me, but there was a car next to him now, a green Lexus, and it wasn't giving him room to move. He swerved into its lane, rammed it, but it recovered and held steady. Who was driving that car? Horns around us started blaring as drivers tried to avoid our erratically zigzagging vehicles. I bobbed up, peered into my rearview mirror, out through the gaping hole in my rear window, and saw that the passenger door of the sedan had swung shut. But I couldn't see Laurel.

Please God, let her not have fallen out, I prayed silently, ducking back down. I slowed to a crawl, compelling

Grasso to reduce speed or hit me full force. Glancing at the guardrail, I had a moment of real panic as I realized it was only about thirty inches high and it wouldn't take much more than a nudge to pitch me over it into the mud-brown waters below. Water-phobic that I am, the thought of sinking into the depths of the Hudson inside a car slowly filling with polluted river was enough to make me break out in a rash, which is what I do in life-threatening situations.

The Lexus was forcing Grasso against the rail now, and I braced myself for the inevitable crash. When it came, it bashed in my rear end and threw my Honda onto the wide right shoulder a hundred feet or so before the tollgate. In the few seconds it took me to make sure all my body parts were intact, I saw that the sedan had stopped behind me and the nose of the Lexus was wedged into its rear fender.

Grasso was out of his car, but in the time it took him to dash around to the passenger side and yank Laurel up from the floor, I was out of my car, sword in hand. Laurel must've had her hands locked around the seat lever, because it cost him precious seconds to pry them loose. By the time he had her out and was lifting her with one arm to use her as a shield, I had my feet firmly planted and both hands gripping the sword, which was poised over his gun hand. The gun was pointed at the driver of the Lexus, who, with pistol drawn, was crouched behind the rear of his car. By a turn of events totally beyond my comprehension, the man had turned out to be Tomo Yoshida.

"Drop it or she's history," Grasso shouted at Yoshida. I heard the thud of Yoshida's weapon as it hit the ground.

"You drop it," I commanded Grasso, praying he

wouldn't notice either my trembling hands or my squeaky voice. I cleared my throat and added with a bravado that I hoped sounded menacing, "I've always wondered whether cutting off the hand of a thief actually does serve as a deterrent."

His eyes flicked to me and then focused back on Yoshida.

"Get out of my way," he snapped, "or I'll shoot both your Japanese cop friend and Little Miss Busybody here."

Japanese *cop*? I didn't have time to try and make sense of that, because Grasso obviously hadn't bought the scenario that I was going to cut off his hand. Neither had I, but it pissed me off that he was able to take advantage of my lack of killer instinct. I was trying to figure out what to do next when I noticed that Laurel's forehead was streaked with blood and she had a really mean-looking bruise on her cheek. My anger mounted. Until now she'd been hanging limply as though dazed by the crash, but I saw her eyes open and she seemed to be signaling me. I took a step back as she suddenly came to life and delivered a smashing blow to Grasso's gun hand. Yoshida hit the ground as the gun discharged and went flying. Laurel twisted out of Grasso's grasp and went for it, and as he grabbed for her, I did a very unprofessional, unbiofeedback-therapistlike thing. I kicked him right on his injured coccyx. He fell heavily and rolled, groaning, onto his back. By the time he'd recovered his breath, I had the sword suspended over him and I was feeling reckless enough to do some real damage.

"Don't tempt me!"

He lunged for the sword.

I slammed my foot down on his chest, and his hand came away from the blade bloody.

"Why'd you do it? For money? How much money is enough for people like you?"

He shook his head, pressed his hand against his chest to stem the flow.

"What was it? Was Forester going to rat on you? She threaten to tell Laurel you forged her father's will?"

It was a wild guess, but I could see from the expression that passed quickly across his face and then was gone that I'd struck gold. Out of the corner of my eye, I saw Yoshida scramble to his feet, grab the gun from Laurel's hand, pick up his own, and train it on Grasso. Clearly, he didn't have much faith in my swordsmanship, but he didn't make a move to interfere. A crowd had begun gathering, but they kept their distance.

I was on a roll. "I'll bet you thought Helena told Laurel all about the forgery that day in Franny's shop. But she didn't. You killed her for nothing."

"Not—for nothing—there was no reasoning—she was —out of control. She—" He stopped, a grimace contorting his features."

"*What?*"

"She was going to leave a note saying—saying I killed Juliana."

I took another shot in the dark. "You were there the night Juliana died. Laurel heard you and Helena talking."

"It was over by the time I got there," he whispered, "before Helena called me even. She—she'd fed Juliana the pills when Juliana was so groggy she didn't know what she was doing."

I heard movement beside me and knew it was Laurel, knew she'd heard his words.

"So you decided to profit from my mother's murder."

"There was nothing I could do. I couldn't bring her back."

"What was your price? I'd like to know how much my mother's life was worth. I'd like to know what it took to buy your silence."

He didn't answer. Laurel kicked him hard in the side and he groaned again. "How much?"

"Helena paid my law loans and set me up in practice," he gasped. "I thought that was the end of it, but no matter what I did for her over the years, it was never enough. I was never safe. When I married Walawon she swore she'd make me pay."

"What did you do for her over the years?" I asked. "Make her rich by buying and selling innocent little girls? Or were little girls your own particular brand of perversion?"

"It was a business. I only took care of the money end. She handled the other part."

"A business!" Laurel spat. "You scum, you're as guilty as she was." She aimed another kick, but I elbowed her aside. There must be a bit of the killer or at least the bully in me after all, because I did something really outrageous.

"You know, Laurel," I said conversationally, "I think the only way to stop this piece of garbage from doing any more damage with that thing is to remove it permanently." And I allowed the tip of the sword to drop half an inch lower.

He jerked backward, his face becoming purple and ugly with rage. Had I ever thought him attractive?

"I should've gotten rid of you and that stupid old lady when I had the chance," he snarled. "Ball-busting bitch, if it weren't for your interfering . . ." I danced away as he made a grab for me, curses spewing from his mouth like the blood spurting from his wound.

Now, I may be a lot of things, but a ball-busting bitch isn't one of them. If I were, Rich'd be talking in falsetto and I'd be a helluva lot richer. Off in the distance there were sirens and voices shouting, but the sounds didn't really register. A sort of white-hot fury seized me as images whirled before my mind's eye, images of the Thai mother sobbing over the coffin of her fifteen-year-old daughter—a child not much older than my Allie; of Sophie's terrified scream as the thug tried to drag her into his car, this car, Grasso's car; of Laurel's bruised and bloody face as she listened to the way her mother had died.

I lost it. I raised the sword, my hands tightening on the hilt. I swear I was within an inch of becoming what he was calling me when a familiar hand closed over mine and Ted's calm voice was murmuring in my ear, "Stop, Carrie. It's over. I'll be damned if you haven't done it again. Let go of the sword. Let go. It's over."

EPILOGUE

·❋·

> *"The threatened cloud has passed away,*
> *And fairly shines the dawning day:*
> *Then let the throng*
> *Our joy advance,*
> *With laughing song*
> *And merry dance,*
> *With joyous shout and ringing cheer,*
> *Inaugurate our new career!"*

THE AUDITORIUM WAS FILLED with the sound of jubilant young voices as they energetically frolicked through *The Mikado*'s finale.

It was opening night. Ted, Matt, and I were in the third row center of the high-school auditorium. I was on my feet, pounding my hands together, basking in the reflected glory of my beautiful young daughter, who was without question the most delightful Pitti-Sing to ever grace a stage. Alec Roderick was a handsome and charming Nanki-Poo, and Sophida Maitini, an adorable Yum-Yum. Allie had been right about the sweetness and purity of her voice. This was a young woman with a future, and Laurel, who would eventually be coming into her inheritance, was committed to making sure she would get the opportunity.

Allie had accepted her demotion with grace, but I knew that the time Nanki-Poo had spent consoling her over the past two weeks had had a good deal to do with it.

My hands ached from clapping when the final bows were taken and the curtain descended. I turned to Ted. "Weren't they wonderful?"

He leaned over and kissed my cheek. "Fantastic. But Allie stole the show."

I glowed. "Everyone was good, but she was exceptional, wasn't she?"

He smiled. "And a knockout in that kimono and red sash." He turned to my son. "What'd you think of your sister, Matt?"

Matt grinned. "She did okay, I guess."

I laughed. "High praise." My eyes searched the audience anxiously. "Mattie, have you seen Dad?"

He shook his head. "Want me to look around?"

"Would you, honey? Allie'll be so disappointed if he didn't show. Meet us backstage in ten minutes." I turned back to Ted. "God, he really missed something if he wasn't here. She was good."

"Must get it from you," Ted said.

"From me? I don't have any talent. I can't sing."

"You have other talents."

I laughed. "Flattery will get you everywhere."

"Good, because I have a proposition for you."

I still had two and a half months till his birthday. What was this about?

I was saved from whatever it was by Meg and Kevin,

who came bustling up followed by Inspector Yoshida, Franny, and Laurel.

Meg hugged me. "She was wonderful. You must be busting at the seams."

Kevin leaned over and kissed me. "Just beautiful. Like mother, like daughter."

Inspector Yoshida took my hand and bowed over it. "Ms. Carlin, you have an extraordinarily talented daughter. One doesn't expect such a professional job from youngsters doing community theater."

"Thank you. And weren't Franny's costumes gorgeous?"

Everyone agreed, and Franny giggled and blushed like one of the three little schoolgirls in the show at the praise showered on her.

"What happened to the samurai sword?" Laurel asked. "That cardboard thing left a lot to be desired."

Ted laughed. "I think Mr. Creighton heard about Carrie's little run-in with Mr. Grasso. Decided not to take any chances with his own valuables, considering he gave Yum-Yum back to Sophie."

"I should've finished the job," I muttered. "Grasso'll probably buy himself a dream team and walk."

"Oh, I don't think so," Ted said. "Murder, forgery, money-laundering—with what Laurel's organization has uncovered and what we've got from Inspector Yoshida and our informant in the gang, the evidence against him is pretty substantial."

"My office has been working for quite some time trying to stop the buying and selling of women," Yoshida said. "One does wonder what would have made a man like Grasso agree to be a party to it."

"Once he'd made the decision to cover up Juliana's

murder, he'd sold his soul," Ted replied. "He was Forester's boy from that day forward."

"Still," I said. "She obviously planned to marry him after Laurel's father's death and he wouldn't do it."

"His Waterloo. His marrying the young and beautiful Walawon drove her over the edge. The outcome was he had to kill her to shut her up."

Yoshida sighed. "Ah, what a tangled web we weave . . ." he quoted.

I turned to Yoshida. "One thing I've been wondering about. When you came to my office, were you following Grasso or me?"

He smiled. "I was following him and trying to protect you and Mrs. Gold. He made it easier when he decided to become your patient."

I looked at Ted. "Why do you suppose he did that? He knew I was seeing you."

"Nice way to keep tabs on the progress of the investigation," Ted said.

Grasso's words came back to me. *"I'll rely on you to keep me up to date on his progress."*

"I never talk about anything you tell me," I said indignantly.

"Especially," Ted teased, "what you don't know, like the fact that Inspector Yoshida here was working with us."

"You mean, you knew from the beginning who he was and you let me go on thinking—"

"I'd've told you if you needed to know," Ted replied calmly.

"I did need to know." I was seething. There was an uncomfortable silence. I smiled sweetly. "What was that about a proposition you had for me?"

He grinned. "Somehow I don't think this is the moment."

Kev, the peacemaker, jumped in. "I just got back from Key West. Bring me up to date. What've you found out about Forester's will?"

"Grasso's admitted it's a forgery. He used the name of a dead colleague for the lawyer who drew it up."

"Wasn't that taking an awful chance?" Meg asked. "He'd've had to come up with witnesses."

"Only if someone named in the will contested, and neither he nor Klinger would have. As the ultimate beneficiary, Laurel was hardly in a position to contest. He needed to set her up as the killer, and he almost succeeded."

"Why was he trying to kill her, then?" Franny asked.

"He'd found out she'd been poking into the sex-tour thing, had even made contact with the yakuza, who were getting protection money. If he could have eliminated her and made it look like a gang hit, he was home free. The phony tattoo on his hand, the chalked stars— all part of an elaborate scheme to cover his tracks."

"What about the attack on him?" Kev asked. "How'd he manage that?"

Still miffed, I felt a degree of satisfaction watching Ted squirm as he explained.

"The truth was, no one saw the actual attack. He was found wandering, dazed, with a bump on his head the size of an egg. Self-inflicted, but because he was famous and well-respected, I'm afraid we bought his story. At least, initially." He draped an arm over my shoulder. "His problem was he didn't count on Curious Georgette here."

I wriggled away. "I'm going backstage. I want to hug

my daughter and congratulate Mr. Creighton and the cast."

I headed for the dressing rooms with Ted following. As we rounded the corner, he pulled me behind a low-hanging curtain.

"Okay, let's talk."

"About what?" I asked innocently. "Your lying to me? I'm used to liars. I just don't plan to marry another one."

"Wait a minute, now. My not telling you everything isn't lying."

"It is to me."

His expression hardened. "Deal with it. I'm a cop. I'm never going to discuss everything I'm doing with you. If you can't tell the difference between that and a lie, then we've got nowhere to go in this relationship."

I was about to snap at him that that was just fine with me, when Meg's words in the hospital came back to me. " . . . *nutcase who keeps putting her head in the noose . . . something he can live with and still love and want you . . . because you love him his flaws don't seem like flaws . . . what love's all about . . . isn't utopia, but it's a workable relationship.*"

I held my tongue, looked down at my shoes, then back up at his face. It was a nice face. An honest face. I liked it. I liked this man. A lot. I was not going to mess up. I was going to take Meg's advice and lose the old baggage I'd been dragging around. I looked into his eyes, which went from angry slate-gray to a softer shade, sort of the color of Horty's fur, as he read my expression.

"I suppose I'll have to deal with it," I whispered. "On one condition, though."

"Yeah? What's that?"

"That you deep-six Curious Georgette forever."

"Done. I'll have to think of something else."

"Actually, I've been answering to Carrie for quite some time now. Or you could go with Wonder Woman —or Goddess. . . ." I slipped my arm around his waist. "Now, what was that about a proposition?"

He pulled me to him and we walked, arm in arm, toward the dressing rooms. "What I had in mind—my darling Goddess—was a kind of premarital situation, one in which we take a page from the younger generation's book. You know, live together for a while, share expenses, see if we can stand each other on a day-to-day basis, see where it leads. . . ."

I didn't even hesitate. "Sounds good to me," I said.

From backstage came a chorus of young voices reprising the finale.

"The threatened cloud has passed away,
and brightly shines the dawning day;
What though the night may come too soon,
We've years and years of afternoon!"

Match wits with the bestselling

MYSTERY WRITERS

in the business!